# T]
# SECOND
# BLACK BOOK
# OF
# HORROR

### Selected by Charles Black

# Mortbury Press

Published by Mortbury Press

First Edition

2008

This anthology copyright © Mortbury Press

All stories copyright © of their respective authors

Cover art copyright © Paul Mudie

ISBN 978-0-9556061-1-3

Mortbury Press
Shiloh
Nantglas
Llandrindod Wells
Powys
LD1 6PD

mortburypress@yahoo.com
http://www.freewebs.com/mortburypress/

# Contents

*Dedicated to Mary Danby*

\*\*\*\*\*

Acknowledgements

Black Glass © by Gary McMahon 2008
Amygdala © by David A. Sutton 1998 First published in
*Kimota* #9
Now and Forever More © by David A. Riley 2008
The Cold Harvest © by Steve Goodwin 2008
All Under Hatches Stow'd © by Mike Chinn 2008
On the Couch © by Craig Herbertson 2008
The Crimson Picture © by Daniel McGachey 2008
Squabble © by D. F. Lewis 1993 First published in *Bizarre
Bazaar* (USA)
The Eye in the Mirror © by Eddy C. Bertin 2008
The Meal © by Julia Lufford 2008
Onion © by L. H. Maynard & M. P. N. Sims 2008
In Sickness and… © by John Llewellyn Probert 2008
The Pit © by Rog Pile 2008

The Tempest by William Shakespeare

Cover artwork © by Paul Mudie 2008

\*\*\*\*\*

Also in this series:
*The Black Book of Horror*
*The Third Black Book of Horror* (forthcoming)

# BLACK GLASS

## Gary McMahon

She was out there again, the little Goth girl. Pope could see her, leaning lazily against the bonnet of her black Mini Cooper and smoking a cigarette. This was the third night in a row, and her presence, rather than acting as a threat, was becoming something of a comfort. If she was out there, the world was moving along nicely, people were caught up in their petty affairs, and the natural laws of supply and demand were operating as they should.

Pope moved away from the bedroom window and slipped on his silk robe, enjoying the sensation of the material gliding across his naked torso. He glanced at his watch: it was 1.00 a.m. Didn't the girl ever sleep?

Entering the living room, he stood in the doorway and admired for the hundredth time his surroundings. The house was impressive; it never failed to promote in him a sense of awe, and of pride that he was in a position to be able to buy such a property.

Leaving off the light, he drifted across to the main feature: the huge west wall that was composed entirely of glass. It was an architectural victory of form over substance, and the logistics of it all baffled him. How on earth had the builders managed to leave out a load bearing wall and substitute it with glass? Yes, it was thick – perhaps two or three inches – but surely it wasn't as strong as bricks and mortar?

Pope's mind boggled; he was a businessman, and such artistic or technical matters never failed to confuse him. If it was making money you were interested in, then Pope was your man, but if your line was something more creative, then you'd better go elsewhere.

His ex wife, Savannah, was the artistic one; perhaps that was why the marriage had failed. While she thought nothing of spending his money, in her spare time she expressed the

5

vulgarity of their wealth and spent hours weaving baskets or making pots. It was not something Pope could ever understand, nor did he want to.

He watched the girl as she stubbed out her smoke on a fencepost. She turned to face the house, watching for movement; looking for signs of life in the dead of night. He smiled, enjoying the sense that she could not see him watching her. It appealed to his voyeuristic nature – another aspect in which he and Savannah had differed: her idea of sex was pretty conventional, whereas he enjoyed more *visual* stimulation...

The girl stepped forward and leaned against the fence that separated his property from the narrow lane on which she had parked. He could just about make out the white blob of her face in the darkness, the dark blur of her black-clad body. He'd never seen her close-up, but something about her sent shivers along his thighs. There was something sensual about the way she moved, and certainly something compulsive in the way she spied on the house, watching and waiting... but for what? Eddie Woe was dead; everyone knew that. His overdose had made all the national news, and there'd even been a documentary made about his last hours on earth.

Pope scratched his chest, rubbing the warm flesh. The girl did not move.

Since moving into the house, Pope had entertained several unwanted visitors: longhaired youths who'd scaled the fence in search of souvenirs, overweight magazine photographers after a shot of the place where the lead singer of the proto-punk band Nefandor had died, a persistent female fan who kept leaving white roses outside the main gates until the police had cautioned her.

But this girl – the one who arrived during darkness and only left when the sun came up – was different from the usual acolytes of misery. For one thing, she never tried to gain entrance to the property. She just stood there, always in the same place, looking up at the huge glass wall, as if waiting for some kind of display.

Pope smiled, an idea suddenly occurring to him.

He backed away from the window so that he was standing in plain sight as long as it wasn't too dark to see inside the room. The drapes were already open; he liked to be able to watch her with his view unimpeded.

Pope undid the belt of his robe and let the garment fall to the floor. He kicked it away, smiling. Then he clapped his hands twice – the signal for the automated lighting to come on. The room was suddenly filled with a bright white glare, bright as daylight; harsh as a school mistress. He knew that once the lights were on, the girl would be able to see inside – her view of him would be unimpeded. For his part, the window suddenly became a vast black mirror, reflecting him in his glory along with the room surrounding him. He was pleased to note that he was fully aroused; this was the most turned-on he'd felt in months, probably since the divorce.

He couldn't see the girl, so her reaction to the eyeful he was offering would go unseen. Still, it was a price worth paying.

He clapped his hands three times, briskly, and saw a flicker of stealthy movement behind him, over his left shoulder. The lights went off; the window glass turned back from an opaque reflective surface into transparent one. Pope was disappointed to find that the girl was no longer there. He couldn't even see her little car moving off along the road because of the shaggy trees that obstructed his view.

Pope turned away from the window, feeling obscurely snubbed. He glanced into the corner, where he thought he'd glimpsed motion, but, of course, there was nothing there. He went back to bed, attempted, and failed, to masturbate, then slept uneasily for the remainder of the night.

Next day the weather was dull, the sky overcast. After a light breakfast Pope went for a walk around the property, enjoying his new domain.

Ever since he was a young boy, he'd wanted to own a big house on the moors. It was a romantic notion, and one he'd almost dismissed, until his clothing factory had made enough money to realise this stalled ambition. Now that he owned the place, he was unsure of what to do with it; but for now, he was content to wallow in the feeling of having fulfilled a mission first formulated when he lived with his oversized family in a tiny back-to-back in a grubby southern suburb of Sheffield.

From his current vantage point, the house looked even more impressive. It was sleek and modern, yet managed to retain a depth of character possessed by older buildings. There was a sense of permanence here, of the thing having sprouted from the ground rather than being physically constructed.

"And all paid for by shitty rock music," he said, smiling. Pope had no time for modern popular culture, unless there was money in it for him. His clothing label consisted of cheaply made generic outfits that were shipped to specific outlets – mainly pound shops and budget chain stores. His designers merely ripped off whatever look was 'in' that season, and cut their cloth to fit, so to speak. Minimum creativity: maximum profit.

He tried to think of a tune by Nefandor, but all that came to mind was a dirge he'd once heard in a crowded pub during a party Savannah had dragged him along to, something to do with the arty crowd she often socialised with. It meant nothing to him, that racket: it came from a world he didn't even recognise, a place of leather and piercings and sub-culture and counter-culture and a clear disrespect for finance.

"Excuse me."

Pope was so caught up in his own thoughts that at first he didn't hear the voice.

"I'm sorry to disturb you…"

He turned around, his eyes settling first on the black Mini Cooper and then the girl who'd spoken to him. Recalling his antics of the night before, he felt suddenly embarrassed, but then his habitual manner kicked in and he was all smiles.

"Sorry. I don't mean to be a nuisance, but are you the new owner?" She was standing behind the fence, hands in the pockets of torn jeans, sunglasses covering her eyes despite the grey skies and heavy dark clouds.

"Yes. Yes, I am. I'm afraid that all of the rock musician's stuff was shipped out long before I moved in, so I can't help you with anything relating to him."

She smiled; it was such an enigmatic expression that Pope was confused by it, wondering what it meant.

"If that *is* what you're interested in, of course."

She shook her head; thick strands of long jet-black hair fell from her ponytail, obscuring her narrow, high-boned cheeks. "No. Nothing like that. I used to know Eddie and his wife, that's all. I've been here many times before."

"Really? You visited here often?"

The girl's pale face coloured slightly; beneath the kohl-lined eyes, her cheeks bloomed. "Sort of. I used to live here, with Eddie and Eva."

"Eva?" Pope was nonplussed; he knew almost nothing about the former owners other than they were rock stars.

"Eva was Eddie's wife. She went missing before he died."

Pope didn't know what to say, so he let instinct guide him. "Would you like to come in? For a coffee, I mean. Have a look round the old place, relive some old memories?" He didn't know why he was inviting the girl inside, but whatever impulse he was acting upon felt right. He realised for the first time that he was lonely.

"Sure," she said, shrugging her shoulders. "Shall I come round to the gate?" She prodded the barbed wire running along the top of the fence with a long, thin finger. Her nails were painted black, and were sharpened to points.

"I'll let you in," said Pope, and turned away from her, heading towards the main entrance. As soon as she was out of sight, he missed her. She might be small, but she had real presence, like a movie star or a minor member of royalty. She *occupied* space rather than simply taking it up.

He led her up to the house in silence, unsure of what to say now that he'd let her in. She kept a few paces back, as if studying him, and it made him feel uncomfortable. The voyeur had become the viewed.

"This way – but I'm sure you already know that."

She smiled at him as he shifted to one side to allow her access into the house, and her step was light as she walked across the threshold. From behind, she was a wonderful sight: narrow shoulders, trim hips, and a small, firm backside. He watched her as she mounted the stairs to the first floor living quarters, enjoying the way the tight denim jeans hugged her slight curves, the way she moved with an unconscious grace.

"Would you like a drink?" Pope headed straight for the kitchen area of the open-plan living space, taking two glasses from a high shelf.

"You got any brandy?"

He raised his eyebrows, and nodded his head.

"I like brandy," said the girl, shrugging off her coat and collapsing into a chair as if she belonged there – and Pope realised that she did, even more than him.

"What's your name?"

He brought through the brandies, placing one on the table in front of her and taking a sip from the other. "Alec Pope. What's yours?"

She leaned forward and placed a fingertip inside the glass, running it around the rim before plunging it into the brandy. Then she slowly lifted it out of the glass and brought it up to her mouth. Lips parted, tongue sticking out in a small pink point, she placed the finger in her mouth and smiled. "My name's Henna."

Pope sat down in a chair opposite, feeling suddenly clumsy and graceless in the company of this odd creature. She was so far out of his usual social sphere that he viewed her as a rare and exotic animal. He was used to spending time with stiff-haired women in business suits, going on blind dates with identikit versions of the same dull model, so Henna was something new, something alien in his life.

"So. How did you know the previous occupants?"

She smiled. "That's a funny way of phrasing it."

He said nothing, just smiled at her gently mocking tone.

Henna took a mouthful of her drink, then put down the glass. Her lips were wet. "Like I said before, I used to live here, in this house. I stayed here for over a year, and left when things got a bit tricky between Eddie and Eva."

"In what capacity did you stay here? Were you a guest? An employee?"

She giggled; it was incredibly enticing, and Pope found himself attracted to the petite girl in a way that he'd not quite expected.

"A bit of both, really. Some people would call me a groupie, but Eddie and Eva called me their muse. We loved each other, you see. All three of us."

Slowly the salacious implications of this dawned on Pope, and he hid his face behind his hand, keeping the glass to his mouth until he felt safe enough to lower it.

"Does that shock you? The fact that I was with them both." Her smile was flirtatious, a come-on if ever he saw one. She stretched out her short legs, kicking off her boots. The socks beneath were filthy, but it took away nothing from her earthy appeal. She curled her toes, and Pope stared at her feet, wondering what they looked like naked.

"No. I'm not as uptight as I might appear. I've seen and done a bit in my time." He knew he sounded lame, like someone's middle-aged father trying to act cool, but that's what she did to him: made him feel confused and awkward and out of his depth.

Her smile was maddening. He wanted to move over there, slip his arm around her and draw her close... or, better still, he wanted to watch her from afar, scrutinise her without her even knowing.

"I'd better go." She bent over and put on her boots, stood, leaning all of her weight on one hip.

"Will you... would you come back? For dinner?"

She paused, thinking over the invitation. Her eyes shone, betraying the fact that she was still toying with him like a cat tormenting a mouse prior to the killing blow.

"I like you, Pope. You're a weird old geezer... so, yes, I'll come for diner. Tomorrow night. Cook me something nice. Something special."

She stood on her tiptoes and kissed him chastely on the cheek, but as she pulled away she poked out her tongue and licked the side of his neck. "Tomorrow, then."

"Yes," he said, stunned. "Tomorrow."

"Don't worry; I'll let myself out."

Pope spent the rest of the day ghosting around the house, putting things straight, adjusting his shelves, sorting through papers and organising the files on his laptop. He'd told his P.A. that he should not be disturbed, but she'd sent him several updates by email. Things were moving along nicely at the clothing factory; his assistant manager, Mike Jessop, was handling things well. If he kept up the good work, the lad might be in line for a pay rise.

Out of interest, Pope ran an online search for anything relating to Eddie and Eva Woe, and called up over two hundred thousand results. He narrowed it down by entering a reference to Henna. Amid innumerable mentions of henna tattoos, he saw a link to an article about a song called 'Handy Henna', one of Nefandor's biggest hits. He'd never even heard of it. Scrolling down the online lyric sheet, he was both shocked and aroused to discover the highly sexual content of the song.

His mobile rang, drawing his attention away from the laptop, and he fumbled it from beneath a cushion on the sofa. He saw by the display that it was his ex wife calling, and after only a short pause he answered.

"Hello, Savanah."

"Alec. How are you? Did the move go well?"

"Yes, it went fine. Everything's just about sorted."

There was a short pause, during which he could almost sense her organising her words before she spoke. "So," she continued. "It's as nice as it looks on TV? The house."

"It's a marvellous place, one that I'm sure will increase in value."

Savannah laughed, and the sound was so familiar that it was like a series of tiny pinpricks in his heart. Despite their many differences, and the pressures that had driven them apart, Pope had never really stopped loving her and the fact that she still kept in touch spoke volumes regarding Savannah's own feelings towards him – sometimes, he wondered why the hell they'd ever let things get so out of hand.

"Same old Alec: obsessed with commerce."

"You know me. I always did have an eye for business."

"Have you even listened to any of Nefandor's music? Be honest."

Pope laughed. "You know me *too* well. Of course I haven't; I'm more Mahler than Motorhead."

"And that reference alone ably demonstrates your incredible lack of knowledge when it comes to popular music, old boy."

She waited until they'd both stopped laughing at him before continuing.

"They were quite a seminal outfit, you know; a big deal in the world of alternative music. David Bowie discovered Eddie Woe busking on a sidewalk in New York and helped produce the band's debut album. A lot of famous musicians worked with them; even more *wanted* to work with them."

"You don't say…" Pope picked up the remote control and turned on the television, muting the volume. He watched the news while Savannah spoke, remembering why they'd not lasted, the gulf between them – their opposing tastes and interests – appearing all over again.

"Yes. And what's more interesting is that Eva Woe was the creative force behind it all. She wrote all the lyrics, composed a lot of the music; Eddie was little more than a talented front man, a heavy-metal crooner."

"Mmm. Yes."

"Are you even listening, Alec?" She knew he wasn't; he

13

never did. But she put up with him, even now, tolerating his maddening lack of awareness of her needs.

"Sorry, Sav. I'm a little preoccupied. Things on my mind, you know? Was there a reason why you rang – other than just a chat, I mean?"

"Okay, I'll come out with it. I've met someone, Alec. Someone nice. An artist. I wanted you to hear first, before any of your office cronies spilled the beans."

For a moment Pope's heart seemed to swell, as if filled with air, then instantly deflated. It was a curious sensation, and not one he'd ever experienced before. His heart was a little too old and weathered to have broken, but he felt sure that at least a fracture had occurred.

"Alec?"

"Ah. Yes. Thanks for letting me know in person. It would've been hideous to be told by one of my staff, or a mutual friend over cocktails. I appreciate it, Sav. I really do."

More silence; this time it seemed meaningful.

"You know I'll always care for you. Some things can't die; they hang on, probably forever. I'll never do anything to hurt you…" Her words, however well-meant, sounded too much like pity for Pope to bear. He gripped the mobile phone tightly, wishing that he could end the call but too lost in the moment to simply press a button.

"I… I've met someone, too. Yesterday." He regretted his compulsive confession immediately after saying the words.

"Really?" Savannah's voice rose by an octave; she sounded like she'd been let off the hook.

"It's… it's early days, yet. I mean, we've only just had one date – not even that, really. She's coming over for dinner tomorrow night." He was blustering and they both knew it; backtracking, trying to take back what he'd already said. "It's nothing too heavy."

"I'm glad for you, Alec. Truly. Who is she? Would I know her?"

He couldn't help but laugh, and immediately regretted doing

so.

"What? Come on, tell me." Savannah sounded slightly hurt, but almost managed to hide it.

"She used to know those rock stars. She stayed here as a house guest for a while – that's how we met: she was hanging around outside." Pope was digging himself deeper into a hole. Instead of deflecting Savannah's pity, he was generating even more of it. He could feel her caring vibrations coming through the phone, soft hands stroking his cheeks.

"Oh, Alec. Do be careful. How old is this girl?"

"Listen, Savannah, I really do have to go. I have work to do…" He couldn't even think of a decent excuse, falling back instead on an old, well-worn favourite.

"Just promise me you'll be careful, Alec. Don't rush into anything foolish."

"Goodbye, Savannah. I'll ring you next week. We can have lunch – bring your new artist friend." And with that, he finally ended the call.

It was growing dark outside; the sky was turning to charcoal slashes and the vast moor was losing itself in the gloom. Pope turned off the silent TV and walked towards the window-wall, taking in the view. It was beautiful: the sun was a red smear on the western edge of the horizon, and the earth looked soft and spongy beneath the gathering weight of night. He watched the darkness gather in small clusters, then invade the scene, blanking out huge sections of the landscape.

He wondered if Henna would resume her nightly vigil, then decided that she probably wouldn't. There was no longer any need; like a vampire, she could enter anytime now that she'd been invited inside.

When it was fully dark he clapped his hands twice, bringing up the lights. The window turned into a mirror, reflecting his sorrowful figure, the sparse furniture, the ultra-modern kitchen appliances, the empty doorways. He must have been mistaken when he thought he saw a pale, narrow oval ducking down out of sight behind a kitchen workbench; and again, when a thin dark shape flitted across the space in front of the open bedroom door.

"Jesus," he muttered. "I'm not old enough to be senile. Not yet." He smiled, but it was forced, faked. Manufactured to reassure himself that he was not losing his mind.

Another fluttering movement caught his eye, this one low down near the floor, then suddenly above his head.

Pope raised his hands to extinguish the lights, and just as he brought his palms together in an aggressive gesture, he glimpsed something impossible in the mirrored glass. A face. A thin white face. And it was looking directly into his eyes, hovering over one shoulder.

*

Henna arrived just before sundown, and after he let her into the house, she stood at the big window watching the sunset. Pope busied himself in the kitchen, mixing martinis; he had no desire to look through that window.

He'd slept badly after retiring to bed last night, kept awake by strange night fears that alternately reared above him and crouched at the foot of his bed. Turning on the lights offered no protection; these spectres dwelt in the brightness.

The lights were on, but Pope felt edgy. He knew that he was safe from whatever vision had plagued him now that he was no longer alone in the room, but still he felt a subtle oppression, a dread presence hanging over him. It wasn't that he did not feel safe in his own home; it was more the fact that this was *not* his home, nor had it ever been. This house belonged to the dead; to the ghosts of a recent past, and a milieu from which Pope was excluded but his mysterious guest had always been party to.

He handed Henna her drink and sat down on the sofa, hoping yet dreading that she might occupy the space next to him. "I hope you like pasta," he said, trying to break the tense silence. "I'm a decent cook, but my skills are limited."

She turned away from the window; he saw her bare back reflected there, the complex straps of her thin black bondage blouse resembling strange markings on her ivory shoulders. She was tiny, like a doll, but there was a strength to her that seemed unfathomable. Her pointed black fingernails tapped the glass; her dark eyelids fluttered; her maroon lips trembled.

In that moment Pope saw her as the muse she claimed to be – he pictured the three-way lovemaking, the naked song-writing sessions, the drink and drug binges that had undoubtedly taken place within these shivering walls. He viewed them all momentarily reflected in her lake-dark eyes – and in the black glass of the window behind her.

"I spent some happy times here," she said, lowering herself onto the floor at his feet. She tucked her legs up under her bottom, like a small child at story time, and sipped her martini. "I can still feel the creative energy, like it's trapped between the bricks and ingrained in the walls. Can you feel it?"

"Yes," he lied, hoping that it made him more interesting, more appealing to this flighty little being.

Her hand strayed up and onto his knee; his flesh trembled beneath her touch. He gulped at his drink, throat dry, parched. Her palm was hot, like fire; her skin burned him in places left cold since long before his divorce.

"When Eva went missing, Eddie curled up into his shell; he climbed into the bottle and the drugs baggy, and didn't come out again. Six months later, he was dead. I came round after she vanished, tried to bring him out of whatever trance he was in – but he sent me away, like he didn't even know me."

"Why did you leave in the first place? If things were so good between the three of you, what happened to send you away?" He was melting at her touch; his flesh ran like liquid, sliding from the bone.

"There were arguments. Fights. Things turned… they turned nasty. Eddie wanted to sell the rights to some songs, let them be used in TV ads. He was offered big, big money."

Her hand rested on his thigh; she shuffled across the

polished floor, drawing closer.

"Eva wrote all the songs – at least, all the good ones. The publishing details all credited E. Woe as the lyricist, and not many people knew that meant Eva: they all assumed Eddie was the artist. But he was just the face of the music, the one who fronted the group. The music was all Eva's; it belonged to her, and she belonged to it. There was no way she'd allow it to be swallowed up by the corporate machine, to be raped and cannibalised by advertising men."

She was right on top of him now, her arms around his calves, tiny breasts pressing against his knees. Then her hands went under his legs, her fingers kneading the tough muscle of his thighs.

"Those halcyon days could never last; I just hoped they might last longer than they actually did." Tears ran down her cheeks, smudging the kohl from around her eyes, creating thin black hollows. "After Eva left, Eddie's lifelong interest in the occult apparently grew stronger and began to consume him. Last I heard before he died, he'd been hosting all kinds of freaky meetings and Sabbaths."

And then she was straddling him, pulling him close, pressing her meagre weight down onto his body and seeking solace in his embrace. Her kisses were hungry, almost obscenely so; her eyes were closed, not even seeing him. Pope didn't care; he took all that she could give, was happy with whatever scraps she might throw from the table.

They moved onto the floor, taking off their clothes, yet unable to break contact in case something was ruined. He was sitting, his back ramrod straight, and she was squatting in his lap. Their breaths were shallow, desperate; their movements harsh, more like fighting than lovemaking. Pope, ever the voyeur, clapped his hands twice and then glanced over her shoulder and into the window, watching the reflection of her back in the glass... the bunching of her muscles... the twitching of her buttocks... the way the sweat ran down her spine... and a face appeared on the back of her head, superimposed like a photographic image, but definitely there, present, immutable. The face was bone-white, thin as a post, and its features were abstract patterns: round black holes for eyes, thin black slit of a mouth.

Pope bit down a scream, pressing his face into Henna's bony shoulder to blot out the vision. When again he looked up, Henna was panting like a horse, her passion almost spent, but his own ardour had been truncated. The face had become a figure; the figure – long, wispy, like a stick of liquorice – floated across the expanse of darkened glass, moving agonisingly slowly, as if through a thick slurry. It spun in a smooth circle, and then came to rest facing him once more. A scrawny arm rose to head-height, boneless fingers formed a small fist, and the thing began to knock on the glass.

Pope screamed "No!" Tearing his hands away from Henna's moist flesh, he clapped three times in rapid succession. The lights went off; the figure was no longer there.

\*

"It's Eva." Henna spoke coolly, calmly, as if they were discussing a luncheon guest. "She's here, still here. Somehow he trapped her in the glass."

Pope was shaken, but he managed to pretend that he'd pulled himself together. He still wanted to impress this wild, sensual creature, and considered the illusion of bravery a good place to start. "What are you talking about?"

"I mentioned about Eddie's fascination with the occult. The Black Arts. Forbidden knowledge. He'd studied it for years, compiling a library of weird texts and learning almost forgotten rituals. He once told me the glass in that window was made by melting down the stained windows of churches where black masses had been held; he said that there was power in the glass, and he only had to find a way of tapping into that power... I thought it was just the usual drug talk at the time, but now I'm not so sure. He said he used a method called

19

scrying to contact something in the glass, something that answered, and demanded a sacrifice."

Pope paced the room, averting his gaze from the window; even with the lights out, he felt threatened by it. Henna sat on the floor by the window, one hand held out before her, fingers splayed against the glass, the ends blanched white and bloodless.

"I can feel it... like it's vibrating, very gently. It's *thrumming*."

Pope took a shot of whisky straight from the bottle, leaned against the kitchen bench, closed his eyes and counted silently to ten. Perhaps, when he finished counting, she'd be gone.

"I have an idea."

No such luck: she was still there, still excited by the whole thing.

"What? What is it?"

Henna stepped across to the table by the door and picked up her bag – a large floppy shoulder bag, made of saggy old leather and lace. She balanced the bag on one knee and made a big show of rummaging inside; then she pulled out a square, flat package.

"I brought you a gift tonight. I know it's not your thing, but I thought you might like to hear some of their music. Some of *her* music." She slid the record out of its protective plastic envelope. The sleeve art featured an illustration of a horned goat standing on its hind legs, playing an electric guitar.

"Subtle," said Pope, feeling more like his old self.

Henna's smile was almost coy. She walked across the room, eyes scanning every corner. "Now you're going to tell me you don't even own a record player."

Pope shrugged his shoulders. "I only have CDs. I can't even remember the last time I bought a vinyl record."

Henna's body went slack; her entire posture altered, making her look old, defeated. The record slipped from her grip and hit the floor, rolling on its edge across the room and finally coming to rest by the window, where it spun before falling face-up. The album was called *Black Glass*, and the irony of the title was not lost on Pope.

"Wait," he said, remembering something. "When I moved in here there was a bunch of old stuff that had been left behind. An old acoustic guitar, some music tapes, paperback books... and a very old-fashioned record player. I'm sure of it."

Henna looked up, her eyes aglow. "Where are they?"

"I stashed them in the garage."

Outside, unlocking the garage doors, Pope glanced up at the living room window. Henna stood there, staring out into the night – or perhaps peering into some world contained within the glass – and for a moment he considered climbing into the car and leaving her there, with her own madness. But then he remembered that it was a shared insanity: it was Pope who had actually seen the figure; Henna simply put a name to the spirit in the glass, and claimed that she knew what to do about it.

Back upstairs, he placed the record player on the floor and plugged it in to the nearest electrical outlet. It was an old machine – outdated by decades, but still willing to function. A green light flashed on, some internal mechanism began to whirr.

"What do we do now? Just play the record?"

Henna placed the album onto the turntable and faced him. She was breathing heavily and her normally pallid cheeks were flushed. Her chest was reddened, too, as if she was sexually aroused, the blood rushing to her extremities.

Pope waited for her to answer.

"This is their debut album, the one that announced them as a force to be reckoned with. Eva always told me she'd poured everything into this record, and that there were hidden messages planted in it for those interested enough to look for them." Her fingers ran along the grooves of the record, caressing them, warming them up for action.

"What, like that old heavy metal record that's said to contain a satanic verse if you play it backwards?" He'd meant it as a quip, a glib comment to demonstrate how absurd he found this whole situation. He'd conveniently forgotten his terror of less than an hour before, and this melodramatic mumbo-jumbo was further distancing him from the image he'd viewed in the glass. The black, black glass.

"*Exactly* like that."

"Oh, come on. You can't really believe this rubbish?"

Henna grabbed him by the forearm, held on tight. She was a lot stronger than she looked, this waif-like girl. "Seriously. It's the kind of joke that would have appealed to both of them. And Eva used to tell me that if anything ever happened to her I could always reach her through this record. Through the private hidden messages she'd left for me."

Pope pulled away, shuffling backwards on his haunches. Then he stood, pursuing safety in a corner of the room. "I'm not doing this. It's ridiculous. I mean, I can go halfway towards believing there's a ghost trapped in the glass of that window, but the rest of this is so outlandish that under different circumstances it would be funny."

Henna stood, approaching the window. In the darkness, she resembled a lithe jungle cat stalking its prey. She made a little circle, then stood before the glass, watching, waiting. Thinking.

Then, slowly, she raised her tiny black-nailed hands. Clapped twice. And the lights came on.

At first there was nothing but the room's reflection, with the two of them waiting in it. Pope watched his face, and was appalled at the fear held there. By stark contrast, Henna was a study in calm detachment; she seemed completely at ease with the unknown.

"Just think of it," she said, her voice low, barely rising above a whisper. "All the money you'll make when you announce to the world that you've found Eva Woe, and that she's writing new music."

Her words were like a prayer; or a hymn to all that he found holy – money, and the pursuit of riches, Commerce. Finance. To hell with art, now she was singing *his* song, and he began to take up its melody, tapping his feet and shaking his mojo...

"They'll be queuing up to work with her – all the modern greats, singing her new songs. And the fans will turn out in their thousands, paying through the nose to see her perform live, or buy her records. It's a cash-cow, a sure-fire route to millions."

And, finally, he was sold on the idea. He crossed the room to where the little record player sat on the floor, bent down, and flicked the switch to start the music. He stayed the motion of the vinyl disc with his hand – a purely impulsive gesture that felt insanely, wonderfully right – and pushed it backwards, against the normal rotation.

As the reverse bars of a weird tune he'd never even heard of yet sounded strangely familiar began to fill the room, Pope watched as a figure shimmered into being, formed out of the very air around them. The figure was not in the room; it was only present in the reflected reality, swirling in the glass like a strange fluid flaw in its construction.

Henna's hips began to move sinuously, her arms twirled at her sides; she mouthed the backward lyrics to the song that seemed to fill the spaces between air molecules. Pope stood in awed silence, watching the display, his voyeuristic tendencies given free rein as the women danced together, one an imperfect reflection of the other, but neither quite sure which was the original and which was the frail copy.

Cracks appeared in the surface of the glass: crazy patterns that bisected the scene, moving diagonally, like drugged-up worms, cleaving the window into several separate pieces. But instead of breaking completely, the window remained in place. The cracks multiplied, becoming a mosaic, a picture made up of a thousand pieces... until finally, the destruction ceased.

Powdered glass dimmed the air like a mist; Henna danced in place, an animated statue; the ghost in the glass stepped forward, at last moving out of her frame, the separate jigsaw pieces of her image coming together, repairing the whole, only when she had descended into the room. The real room.

Pope opened his mouth, said: "Pah!" He had no idea of what exactly he was trying to communicate. All he could do was repeat the absurd sound. He was no longer pushing the record; the backwards music continued playing on its own.

"Pah!"

He stood and took a hesitant step towards the entity that was forming from the floating glass fragments – a beautiful, willowy woman with ash-blonde hair and emerald eyes, whose face was alabaster and body was surely carved from soapstone.

The music stopped.

He took another step... and hit an obstacle. His nose flattened against something cold and hard and immovable; his cheek smeared as he turned his head to see.

The two women smiled at him. He noticed that they were holding hands. Choking back a scream, holding back the truth, Pope began to hammer against the glass. Then he *did* scream, but his voice was hoarse: the sound was dull, mono, like an old record played on an ancient device, all crackles and background hiss.

Henna, his little Goth girl, let go of her companion's hand; her fingers came away reluctantly, as if she never again wanted to release her grip on the thing she loved most in the world, *this* world, *that* world. The world beyond the glass.

She brought up her hands, held them out in front of her face, stretched out her arms. Clapped three times, and the lights went out.

Pope screamed again as the women turned away, dismissing his muted cries and disappearing into the darkened room, but they did not hear him. He pushed himself away from the glass, and turned to survey his new world. Around him was only darkness; his suddenly etiolated limbs moved laboriously, as if through mud. Far ahead, from somewhere deep within the artificially thickened blackness, there came the sound of someone tittering. This was followed by a noise like heavy, dragging footsteps.

Pope waited, hearing distant music that he could not name,

and prepared to meet whatever had just begun to whisper his name.

# AMYGDALA

## David A. Sutton

Dark winter streets are exuding fog. Like it was steam coming off a hot, freshly laid skin of tarmac. And the amber street lamps are hazy, glowing balloons, and the car is crawling along, with its tyres hissing at me as though they were adhering to the road surface. And...

The turnoff negotiated, the old hospital buildings huddle in groups, motionless lumps of grey concrete, or older red brick, with many yellow-lit rectangles covering their surfaces, and narrow five miles per hour maximum access roads weaving in and out and sleeping policemen lying in wait...

And...

People are parking their cars and shuffling forwards under the weight of the fog that is particularly dense hereabouts. They head in the direction of faded, unlit signs over doorways: Accident & Emergencies; Wards 18-32; Intensive Therapy & Theatres 1-4. Many visitors are trudging, like automatons, to their destinations wrapped in thick overcoats and scarves to keep out the cold. I'm reminded of my task tonight and how enormously important it is. Persuading myself to undertake this venture has not been easy, but there came a recent period in my life, a temporary fugue state, out of which emerged a new *me*. One of uncompromising resolve.

Seven o'clock.

Always the best time, early evening. So many relatives visiting the sick and injured, you see. And medical staff changing shifts; caterers clearing up patients' dinner dishes. The hospital particularly busy at this time of the day. So occupied are the staff with their jobs, that I shall likely go unnoticed as I proceed about my business.

The car clicks at me, complaining as its engine cools, and the shrubs in front of where I parked are backlit from a window, reflected in silhouette onto the windscreen. The spray of naked winter branches resembles white nerve fibres, denuded of the internal organ from which they have been stripped. Such an image also reminds me of my obligation.

I slip the white lab coat over my shoulders, button it up and pull a pristine plastic apron on over that. The apron's touch against my fingers is squeaky and moist, the sound reminiscent of a scalpel dividing skin as taut as an inflated balloon. The slithering of my cold fingertips across its surface is sensuously like that of a surgeon's, running his fingers along the slippery, white, fatty tissues that stretch between the displaced contents of an opened abdomen.

The grin in the rear-view mirror is wide and all teeth. Fortunately, the grin cannot see the eyes. The rectangular mirror is too narrow, as if it were made for the purpose, and only the grin reflects. The mouthparts are, after all, the only reliable parts to observe. The lips and the teeth, and the tongue, sometimes plopping into view, provide the entire stimulus I need. The full gamut of emotions is expressed there, captured and *controlled*. They are restricted only by the limitations of the animation available to the mouth. Closed lips, for instance: devoid of feeling. Or open slightly, teeth bared: anger. Tongue peeking out teasingly. Tongue protruding shamelessly, changing its shape, slapping lasciviously. Yes! Chattering teeth: shivering brittle-hard and nervous. Hard enough sometimes to suffer chipped incisors.

The doorway to the soul. That's the mouth. This truth was revealed to me when my dissociation of personality ended.

The grin dominates the mirror and does not allow the eyes to infiltrate. The eyes are not allowed to see themselves. Other mirrors are avoided or positioned accordingly. The eyes are insignificant blobs of jelly and fluid.

Of...

The abstract inside. The untouchable, maddeningly ungraspable parts. The streaming, screaming information bits that you want to lash out at and tear away, severing the many thousands of coiled micro-fibres, ripping their ends from the connections that cannot be seen with the naked eye, but which are there nevertheless, circuits of teasing, corrupt falsehoods.

*I'm ready.*

The mouth is ready, it's *grinning*.

Uncle is at home, waiting *very* patiently.

Tonight is a first and I would be expected to be nervous. Wouldn't you? The mouth expresses the anxiety extremely well and, had I brought a mirror from the car, I would behold my timorousness. Breath is coming out of the mouth, condensing in the frosty night, billows and billows of hot air, more than normal because of the adrenaline and the blood pressure.

Mortuary.

The mouth sees the building…

AUTHORISED STAFF ONLY BEYOND THIS POINT.

A large, open rectangular vehicle entrance looms under the instruction. Darkness fills the space now, the lights are off. But I know the way, my rehearsals have been protracted. My apron squeaks as I walk. More confidently now, I pass through the double swing doors which are really for the trolleys and the medics who push them. Beyond the doors the corridor is well lit, bright with fluorescence.

I realise the need to hide my growing confidence and zeal, thus the fixed grin has reluctantly to be suppressed. I don't need a mirror to show me how appropriately sad and mournful my expression has instantly become. The eyes, I'm not one hundred percent sure about, but they do not really count, treacherous organs that they are.

The empty corridor is wide and cold and along the middle of the grey floor tiles, red directional strips guide the way. So no chance of my becoming lost. Ceiling lights slide past overhead and hum contentedly. Corridors branch off; corridors are like arterial passageways. A service lift with wide horizontal doors expresses itself as a closed, stern mouth. Administrative offices might be empty, except that people are probably hidden beyond the opaque glass panels and the dog-eared notices taped thereon.

The room I want is easy to find, because it smells. Antiseptic clean, but with an under whiff. Detectable decay. Inside it is nearly as chilly as the night outside. Gleaming white enamel slabs in rows wait for occupants. Sluices and drains cry for the gurgle of blood.

There is someone in the mortuary, placing a green plastic sheet over the only other resident, who occupies one of the autopsy tables. The man's gaze transfers its interest to me, confusion exhibiting itself in the curve of the mouth. He sees the white uniform I am wearing, however, and continues his ministrations, although I can detect his unease, because he does not recognise me.

The words he speaks I understand – *who're you?* – but I do not answer. Silence is what I require, because his mouth is not permitted to speak. *Not ever.* And the mouth will only speak when spoken to and then only to reply according to a prearranged script. Otherwise the eyes are likely to assume control and reveal too much of the inside, and the abstract wiring will need tearing out, and cauterising with a red-hot scalpel and clamps.

The mouth is showing its emotion now. I don't need a mirror to tell me that the teeth are naked and ugly looking. Chattering they are, too, just slightly. The breath is coming through with a hissing sound and saliva flits through the gaps in the incisors. The mouth must look pretty threatening.

The man is wrinkling his face all over, but I am not looking at his eyes. There's annoyance displayed in his mouth and I can tell it is about to add something to what it said before. Against all the rules. I raise an open hand in a gesture to stay the sounds before he utters them, but too late – *Who the fuck are you?* – and the effect inside me is excruciating. An abrupt migraine, can you imagine it? *Infuriating.* I will *not* have any words spoken not of my making!

*I'll have to ask you to leave, otherwise I will call security!*
Ow!

He produces a portable two-way radio from the pocket of his laboratory coat, brandishing its wobbly black aerial at me, a feeble weapon.

His pathetic gestures do not matter in the slightest. Fearlessly, the grin becomes deeper and wider, almost agonising, and thundering forwards at a terrific pace, dragging me with it. Next, the man is falling away from me even before I reach him. Fright overwhelms his mouth, so much so that his teeth display themselves as though he has decided to mimic my expression. His radio slithers across the floor, its aerial a stiffened rat's tail. The man's lower back bounces against one of the tables and he whooshes out a breath as one of his kidneys calls out its pain.

*Fucking get away from me...!*

His mouth, widening in fear, sees the instrument trolley, as if he beholds it for the first time, although he undoubtedly placed it there himself. He watches me grab a mixed handful of the stainless gleaming utensils lying neatly in rows. He has slipped onto the floor and his hand goes to his back to tend the self-inflicted kidney punch. He groans miserably, but he's still wildly excited. Scrambling around, he is much as a crab would be with half its legs amputated. I know more articulate sounds are going to come out of him and have to do something to make them stop before the *big* sound comes out. The one that will alert other members of staff.

Unexpectedly, he is curling up into a foetal position and that suits me – *Please don't!* – because now there are no arms or legs to become entangled with, and his mouth can be observed without difficulty and maintained in the manner to which it should be accustomed. It opens obligingly and I stuff inside a large wad of cotton wool I'd brought with me, produced from my trouser pocket while he wasn't looking. I press down firmly, the tongue underneath the wad trying desperately to reverse the manoeuvre with dry, choking coughs, but failing. With the heel of my left hand now placed firmly over his mouth and chin, holding the head against the floor, my right hand uses the instruments. Although, I have to say that I used to be left handed. The utensils are held as you might for plunging a dagger. Then before you know it they are ripping and tearing. They make an unusual multiple tracery across the neck. An aerial map, as it were, of a complex river delta, developing in a tide of living red before evolving messily into a lake on the floor.

The body jerks heavily, legs and arms twitching like a pinned insect.

The mouth grins wide and deep, and I almost wish I had a mirror to enjoy the show.

Now I am free to go about my obligation unhindered, although I must be quick, must be quick, must be quick and the one single occupant in the room will have to do although it is better to have had a wider choice for Uncle. I know there is the man on the floor, but he is still undergoing convulsions, his limbs in spasm and pink froth gushing, and I do not have the time to wait to ensure the abstract wires inside him are completely disabled before I perform.

The operation.

In my white coat, the deep pocket contains a hammer. I lift back the green plastic sheet, hoping against hope for someone young and am blessed tonight with the body of a teenage male. The very ideal requirement in fact. Especially because its eyes are firmly closed and thereby not causing me any anguish.

The mouth grins so broadly now, so joyful with its luck.

The body flips over very easily in my hands, the neck flopping limply, which suggests to the medically trained the probable cause of death. Fortunately, the head itself is undamaged. Had it been harmed, tonight would have been a complete waste of time.

Dry brown hair covers the back of the boy's head. No time for ceremony, I bring the hammer down sharply, centre-stage. Viscous cerebrospinal fluid pours out from the cracked cavity, draining off nicely. I select one of the clean instruments from the trolley and slit through the scalp until I am able to peel it back and separate the broken sections of bone beneath the flesh and open up the interior. Working with the knife, I concentrate on disengaging all remaining obstructions: the stalk of the pituitary and the medulla oblongata from the spinal cord.

Out of my white overcoat, I flourish a clear plastic bag and a pair of rubber surgical gloves. I slip the gloves on, gently scoop out the skull's contents, and place them in the bag, a streak of blood smearing the inside as it goes in, a telltale sign that the organ is quite fresh. Holding the bag up to the light, its contents so unblemished, so malleable and awaiting transformation, is ecstasy.

The grin cannot contain itself now. The mouth even wants to laugh, to shriek with joy, but that desire must be quelled, because it isn't allowed yet. Not yet, not until I have successfully resurrected oblivion.

Steaming fog like it was hot, fresh tarmac and the street lamps glowing amber balloons and the car crawling with tyres hissing as though sticking to the road surface. And...

And the need to maintain a slow and regular speed so that the brain might remain safely on the passenger seat in the plastic bag I have sealed with a bag-tie. There is condensation forming on the inside of the bag with the car's interior warming up, which conceals the brain so no busybody might otherwise see that it resembles something purchased at the butcher's shop.

Pairs of lights cruise past annoyed with my car's slowness, but the smile in the mirror dismisses them. A light smile, a smile of mild disdain. If they had to do the job I was having to, they would also drive with more caution. A big car screeches forward, slowing as it rides next to me on the dual carriageway, keeping pace with my speed. Inside, there is a face that is all mouth, all snarl, and hands are thumping the steering wheel and the driver's mouth is letting forth with expletives that, luckily, I cannot hear through the sound of the engines and the closed windows, and the heater fan.

*Amygdala*

I stop.

And he's through the red light which he didn't see in time and there is a minor accident when his big car clips the rear bumper of another vehicle crossing legitimately in front. Both cars slew sideways, slow down, and recover, but the big car grunts and roars off, although its driver should stop so that both occupants can exchange insurance details.

The mouth in the rear view mirror slaps its lips together in a self-satisfied manner, knowing that such stupidities are beyond it. The outright abandonment of emotion is unthinkable. The wild failure to observe what is going on around is a stupidity of the first order and not permissible.

Home!

The garage door is similar to a mouth opening automatically, a mouth with no tongue and teeth, but instead the car slips inside; a prosthetic metal tongue yet to be coated in flesh.

And…

Uncle is waiting as patient as the dead do wait.

On the dining table.

I've cleared the table of everything except for the white cloth on which he is lying. Uncle looks very small, thin, and frail. He's quite a bit older than I am, so, along with his present status, that is to be expected.

Earlier, I prepared him and now it is a simple matter to lift off the top of his skull which I had sawn away, from the forehead to the middle, a full half-dome of skull in fact. His face is not particularly pale, but his eyes are closed. Uncle's mouth, though, oh, the mouth! A cheeky grin curves his ruby lips, just revealing a thin crescent of white teeth beneath. The smile is frozen there, ready for use.

Soon.

My white lab coat and plastic apron lend a professional air to the proceedings. And they are needed, for this is a solemn and groundbreaking moment in medical history. The first ever brain transplant. All organ replacement surgery before tonight was merely rehearsal!

I am already aware that the brain I have brought with me will not fit inside Uncle's skull cavity and have prepared for that. A plastic washing-up bowl and scalpel have been put out to perform the required excisions. The so-called grey matter has to be cut away; the two hemispheres of the cerebral cortex are superfluous to Uncle's needs. There is too much information in their jelly-like convolutions, too much that is unnecessary, all that ungraspable wiring! I slice away carefully as the brain sits in the bowl, through occipital lobe, parietal and frontal lobes. The offending parts float off in a swirling mixture of fluid and blood, but there is still space in the bowl for me to work and to see that I have reached the crucial areas. I am down to the thalamus, hypothalamus, the cerebellum and reticular formation. Most importantly, *undamaged*, is the mass of neurones of the *amygdala* nestling within the temporal lobe.

It takes one of flexible attributes and forward thinking to accept the importance of the archaic amygdala. Primitive though this early brain is considered, let us not underestimate how powerfully it controls the mouth, the tongue, and the teeth. How dismissive it is of the eyes and the wiring and all extraneous thoughts. The emotion of the mouth is its sole purpose.

Lifting the precious groupings of the remaining brain, I find, delightfully, that the fit into Uncle's skull is as near perfect as it possibly can be. His mouth *almost* moves as I insert the brain into the cavity, and I sense the anticipation waiting there. The teeth snap together satisfactorily. His or mine I'm not sure, perhaps both! Quickly I replace the skullcap and I use fake skin and cauterise and seal the seam with a small soldering tool. Uncle is bald, but that will not be for very long. The smell of singed plastic is pungent and choking, making the mouth display its distaste, but I am not about to allow a bit of discomfort to spoil this illustrious moment.

Gently, with the reverence he deserves, I lift Uncle from the makeshift operating table. He is so frail and light! And yet so uncomplaining – there was, after all, no anaesthetic administered for his operation!

I am drained, almost exhausted by the evening's work, but determined that my perseverance will bear fruit before the night is through. It cannot wait. Sitting in the big armchair by the fireplace, I allow Uncle to rest upon my lap. His legs dangle so limply. He too is exhausted.

Very gently, very kindly, I say to him, "How do you feel, Uncle Charlie?" The mouth knows how to behave in such a delicate situation. "Would you like something to drink?" I ask. I know he must be thirsty after such a lengthy wait.

The fire has gone out while I've been at the hospital and the room has turned chilly. Still, that can be attended to in a moment and Charlie can sit next to me in the chair and we can discuss plans for our future entertainment long into the night. Explore routines and engage in dialogue.

I wait.

The mouth is set, fixed, worried about Charlie's continuing silence, his failure to answer my questions. Yet... yet I know he *will* answer me, that he *is* about to reply. I must give him a little more time. It was a major operation after all. The amygdala must be allowed to recover its self. I try to change my expression while I wait, but the mouth will not let me. Sardonically, it is frozen and I know this is how it must remain – upper row of teeth a fraction exposed, resting on a slightly withdrawn lower lip, a little half-smile – in order to allow Uncle to respond properly.

Now it's coming!

*Now...*

I cannot move for the intense anticipation that is inside me, twisting my innards. The mouth holds me motionless, staring. I wait as seconds tick audibly from the face of the mantel clock.

But...

Something's wrong. There *is* something wrong!

The brain, *the brain is faulty!* The amygdala must be retarded. I am aware of this because of the way the words are going to be spoken. Imbecilic is the term! But how could I have foreseen that the brain became damaged before I got to it? That it was, in fact, the brain of a retard! Even as the last second ticks, I realise with bitter disappointment that I must begin all over again. Despite the truth of this, the mouth will not end its actions and salve my agony and frustration! It insists on allowing Charlie to respond.

Which he does. Determined to answer my question, he is.

"A gottle of geer," he says, mouth clacking dementedly as I support him from inside his back, "a gottle of geer, you gugger and ge hucking kick agout it!"

# NOW AND FOREVER MORE

## David A. Riley

The little village looked somehow frail and insubstantial in the drizzle against the pale grey glow from the sea, as if the spray from the waves that broke against the jagged rocks had momentarily invoked a mirage between the wind-swept hills on either side. The flaking, whitewashed walls of the clustered houses, that stretched around the bay in row after row up the lower slopes of the hills, seemed, if anything, to accentuate this impression of unreality. Daniels shivered, with a feeling of depression, as he stepped with his wife, Julie, down the empty path from the cliffs, his broad face reddened by the winds that lashed into them, tinged with salt. Julie tightened her hand about his as the village came into sight.

"Only one more day," Daniels said in reply to her unvoiced remark. "Then we can go on to St. Auban. I promise. You'll like it much better there, even in weather like this."

When they booked their stay here earlier in the year, neither of them had expected to find this 'unspoiled' village on the Cornish coast to be quite as dispiriting as this. It was not so much the weather, though, they knew, even if this was what they had somehow or other come round to blaming so far since their arrival, nor was it the general quietness of the place, since this was why they had chosen to come here originally. Julie knew that her husband needed a break after all the long hours he'd been putting into work recently. They'd been married for just over two years now and had moved several months ago into their first proper home, after living in a flat above a row of shops in Wolverhampton. After much discussion they had decided that this was what they needed to do if they were to start a family – something which now, to her great relief, they had decided to do. She smiled to herself as she thought of her brother, Arthur. He'd been married just a year longer than them and already he and Lorraine had a two-

37

year-old daughter. She'd enjoyed being the little girl's aunt, but that wasn't enough. She wanted – in fact, she *needed* – a baby of her own.

Julie caught sight of the Broken Mast, where they had a first floor room. She wondered whether it was the atmosphere of that place that upset them so much, as flecks of spray from the bordering quay scattered across the smooth-worn cobbles about their feet as they strolled along the street towards it. The small-paned windows of the Broken Mast gleamed in the pallid light like deep black glossy stones set within its plaster walls. Daniels squared his shoulders as they walked towards it, almost as if he was preparing himself for a distasteful ordeal.

"Let's not go in just yet," Julie suggested suddenly, tugging his arm.

"Why ever not?" Daniels asked in surprise. He was cold already from their walk along the path that meandered across the cliffs, and his trousers were soaked. "Where else can we go in this place?"

A seagull screamed across the sky, gliding with its great white wings outstretched against the buffeting winds beyond the swaybacked roofs of the houses opposite. Their empty windows mirrored the empty lifelessness of the street.

"We could always have a look at the church," Julie suggested hopefully, looking up the street away from the sea to where an unimpressive, stone-built spire rose bluntly above the trees. "We haven't been yet," she continued, "and it does look old. There might be something of interest for us to look at, I suppose. Besides," she said, wrinkling her nose at the inn, "anywhere would be better than that miserable hole."

Quietly they made their way through the village, arm in arm. The sound of the sea died away behind them to a subdued hush as they rounded a bend in the street and started to climb the steep incline from the bay. The church rose almost furtively before them, its stout walls all but hidden behind a grove of elms, whose knotted roots disrupted the even surface of the ancient burial ground.

Julie smiled hopefully as they pushed open the wrought iron gate in the surrounding wall, her face tense against the cold. Daniels knew that she would be better off in the inn, where at least she could get warm. It was senseless trailing here on a day like this. But, he supposed, as he looked around at the lichened and unreadable headstones, leaning at odd angles all about them, it was too late to turn back now.

"It looks quite old," Julie said as she looked up at one of the stained glass windows, in which a bearded saint was depicted frowning at a snake about his feet.

"And neglected," he added heavily, pointing out a hole broken in one of the windows. "The wind probably howls like a pack of wolves through a hole like that."

"It certainly doesn't say much for whoever's supposed to look after it, I suppose," Julie admitted as they peered through the porch into the gloomy interior of the church. A cobweb, silvered with drops of rain, was stretched across one of the upper corners of the arched doorway.

"Shall we go in?" Julie asked, following his gaze across the heavy door.

"We might as well, now we're here," he replied unenthusiastically.

Although the damp mustiness of the air inside the church was unpleasant, Daniels was surprised at how different the atmosphere seemed, almost as if they had somehow stepped out of a clinging fog of depression and were surrounded by clean air at last, which was strangely paradoxical, since the air was certainly no fresher than outside – very much the opposite, in fact – yet, when he looked across at his wife beside him, he could see that this change had obviously been felt by her as well, in the way in which the lines of tension about her frail, sometimes elfin face were visibly beginning to relax as she gazed about herself at the dark interior of the church, her gloved hands gliding appreciatively across the polished wood of the fine old carvings that stood out along the rows of pews.

Their footsteps echoed through the church as they walked down the nave. Daniels' first impressions of neglect were quickly confirmed by the swathes of dust blown into drifts about the paved floor, whilst folds upon folds of grey cobwebs were gathered like discarded blankets between the pews and about the windows. Pointing these out, Daniels said:

"This place hasn't been used for months, perhaps years. The font's full of filth and as dry as a bone, the few cushions still left hanging behind the pews look as if they're ready to fall apart with decay, while the whole place stinks of neglect." He shuddered with revulsion.

Julie stared up at the clotted shadows between the web-draped beams that spanned the ceiling.

"But it's the only church here. How could it have possibly been allowed to fall into disuse like this? It doesn't make sense."

"I don't know. It baffles me too."

Where a cross should have stood on the altar, there was a heap of dried leaves. The altar cloth was stained with blotches of what looked like mildew, and had been tugged violently to one side.

"You'd think someone ransacked the place at some time," Daniels said. He shook his head, puzzled, as he felt at the altar cloth. "Damp," he remarked, letting it go and rubbing his fingers clean on the sides of his coat.

"We surely can't have missed seeing another church in a village as small as this," Julie said.

"Unless they're going to one in the next town."

"But St. Auban's too far away. I can't imagine them travelling all that way."

Beginning to bore of the subject, Daniels wished that he had insisted on returning to the inn, rather than trailing out here. He turned his back on the altar and said:

"We could speculate uselessly for hours and get no nearer the truth. We'd be better off returning to the Broken Mast now while it's dry. With any luck we can have insulated ourselves against the locals with a rose-tinted alcoholic haze before they start rolling in later on."

\*

As they returned into the village, Daniels noticed one of the local fishermen, sat with his back to them by the quay, where he stared with a kind of fixed solemnity across the lines of moored fishing boats that swayed slowly in the waves washing against them. His rounded shoulders and sunken head made the old man look like a large, half-filled sack, over which someone had carelessly thrown an oilskin coat and a dirty, old, woollen cap. Salt-stiffened strands of dank, white hair stuck out from beneath his cap in forlorn spikes. For a moment, as they approached him across the wet cobblestones, he was motionless, deep in thought. Then, slowly, hearing their footsteps, he turned and watched them draw towards him. His thick lips sagged into a scowl, a trickle of saliva appearing in one corner, before he wiped it away with the back of his calloused hand.

"Good evening," Daniels said, as they paused for a moment, breathing in the salty air from the sea as it blew in their faces.

The man grunted something in reply, his eyes passing smugly from Daniels to his wife. Daniels felt Julie's hand tighten about his.

"It's about time this weather started to improve a bit," Daniels went on conversationally, almost gabbling, though he could not have explained why he was making the effort to arouse something like a normal human response from the man. He knew that he might just as well have left him alone for all the good it would do. They had tried on more occasions than they cared to remember in the past few days to start some sort of conversation with one of the villagers. Apart from Marsh, the far from loquacious landlord of the Broken Mast, they had never had anything more than a partial and misleading success. "I notice none of the boats have been out today. I expect

41

you'll be waiting for the weather to improve so you can get in some more fishing."

The man shrugged carelessly, turning away. A smell, like that from an uncleaned stable, seeped into the air. It was a smell which they had begun to grow used to when near the villagers, a smell that all of them were tainted with, to some degree or another. Although they had initially found it repulsive, they had begun, after the first couple of days, to find it just about bearable. Now, though, after the musty but somehow cleaner air of the church, it seemed even worse than before, and Daniels had to grit his teeth against the nausea it produced. The foul creatures probably never even washed, he thought with indignant disgust, a disgust intensified by the careless ease with which the man deliberately ignored them.

"Come on," Daniels said thickly, "we'll get back to the inn. I could do with a strong drink to wash away some of the stench of this place."

Julie's face paled apprehensively as they continued on their way down the street past the old cottages, with their small windows and salt-stained walls. In his anger Daniels had spoken intentionally loudly so that the ignorant old fisherman would hear him. His jaw tightened aggressively, and Julie could tell that his patience with the village and its inhabitants was coming to an end.

"Only one more day, sweetheart," she reminded him as they approached the Broken Mast, its unvarnished, almost featureless sign swinging back and forth in the gusts of wind with a grating, yet melancholy creak.

"One more day!" he grunted, as he pushed open the door into the inn. "And one more night too!"

*

Later that evening, after they had eaten their dinner and retired into the twilit, oak-filled bar for a drink, Daniels said:

"I suppose I shouldn't have lost my temper with that old

42

bastard on our way back from the church."

Circling her hands about a glass of gin and tonic, Julie lowered her head. "He asked for it," she said quietly. "They've no right to be so rude all the time. They act as if anyone from outside their own squalid, little village was somehow subhuman."

Daniels chuckled.

"And yet, if there was ever a group of people I could have possibly had the gall to call subhuman, it would be the inhabitants of this Godforsaken place." He lowered his voice as several of the locals, the collars of their heavy, rain-soaked coats pulled up about their ears, came in and ordered drinks at the bar. "I've yet to see one of these people," Daniels went on, "who doesn't stink, isn't round-shouldered and doesn't have skin that would look coarse on a pig. I suppose some kind of inbreeding could account for the 'local look'. I'd certainly recognise someone from this place anywhere. There's something about them…"

"Something unhealthy?"

"Like a disease? I suppose so, though I don't think that's it. Not exactly. *If*, that is, there's anything to be exact about."

"It's your last night 'ere, I b'lieve?" The voice was guttural and loud. Like that of most of the villagers, its accent was not typically Cornish, though Daniels thought that this sounded Northern in some strange way. Surprised at the interest one of the locals should have in them after having been ignored for so long, and at one of them actually opening a conversation for once, Daniels looked round and said:

"That's right. We're off in the morning. We've booked a room in St. Auban for tomorrow night. We'll be leaving on the midday bus."

The man who had spoken was one of the newcomers, tall but stooped, with a long, almost goatish face that looked sick. His dark blue overcoat dripped with rain and there were stains of what looked like slime about his trousers and cuffs. The hand with which he held his beer was heavily discoloured. Worse

43

still, there was a disturbingly gangrenous look to it, especially at the tips of his fingers as he pushed back the glasses perched on his nose, and said:

"You'll be glad to leave 'ere, I s'ppose?"

Wondering whether he was trying to entice him into some kind of criticism of the village, Daniels said, tactfully:

"You can't judge a place properly in weather like this." Having no intention of making an argument with these people, Daniels realised, perhaps for the first time, just how much he had grown to fear them since their arrival here. It was a realisation which he did not particularly like.

The man smiled, though it was poorly done and seemed deliberately false – insultingly so. Daniels felt the blood start to drain from his face, and he knew that he had gone pale. His hand tightened about his drink.

"We carn't 'elp the weather," the man said matter-of-factly, his jaundiced eyes meeting Daniels' in something of a challenge.

"None of us can help the weather," Daniels replied with a shrug of his shoulders.

The other men, silently drinking their pints, watched on, their flaccidly-featured, pale grey faces showing little interest besides that of a thinly concealed contempt. Degenerate bastards, Daniels thought. There seemed an almost natural animosity between themselves and the villagers, as if there was something about both which the other had no choice but to hate. Not for the first time, he wondered what impulse had prompted him to choose a place like Pennerin Bay for a 'relaxing holiday'. Off the beaten track? Unspoiled? Yes, it was both of these things in a sense, though 'unspoiled'? he wondered. Somehow there was something about the village which told him that it was far from unspoiled. In some way it had been, though he could not see what. Not quite.

Their conversation dying in a still, rather embarrassing silence, it was with relief that Daniels diverted his attention back to his wife, laughing quietly, though without much humour, as he took long drinks of his beer.

The night dragged remorselessly by as more and more of the locals stepped in, the subdued humming of their muttered conversations filling the close atmosphere with a disturbing dissidence. No smiles, no jokes, no sudden eruptions of laughter or argument served to break the dull monotony of their talk. And gradually, as the hour grew late and the sky visible through the tiny windows changed from the slate grey of evening to the claustrophobic blackness of night, Daniels found that his nerves were beginning to fray. There seemed to be more of the locals in the bar tonight than usual, and their collective chatter seemed louder, though hardly more distinct, than before.

"That's your eighth pint," Julie chided as he returned with a drink from the bar.

He placed it over-carefully on the beer-slopped table between them, and said:

"It's the only way to wash away their stench." He remembered having said this several times already during the course of the evening.

"Speak quieter," Julie whispered. "They'll hear you."

"So what? Let them know. Why shouldn't they? They do stink, don't they? I'm not exaggerating." He shut his eyes for a moment, and a black void spun vertiginously in front of him. *What am I saying? Control yourself*, he thought, trying to will himself sober again, though his grip kept slipping. "I'm sorry," he said, pushing his drink away from him. "You're right, it's time I stopped. I've had more than enough already."

"And we've a busy day tomorrow. The bus stops by at twelve, don't forget."

He nodded his head. He wished now that they had brought their car with them, although at the time it had seemed such a good idea to get away from it all and 'learn to use their legs again'. He grunted as he felt a wave of nausea sweep over him.

"I think I'm going to be sick," he muttered. He climbed to

his feet and pushed past the empty table next to theirs and staggered towards the Gents. As he lunged through the door into the toilets, he heard someone step in after him.

"You don't look so good." The voice seemed to float in the air about his head, directionless. He said something in reply as his eyes blurred with an overwhelming nausea. He leant over to his left, and his fingers encountered the cold surface of the single enamel sink. Gratefully he drew himself over it and turned on the taps, drops of water splashing back at his face as he sank towards the basin. Almost detachedly, he wondered if he was going to pass out. Everything was going black, a seething maelstrom of darkness that swirled around and around like the water in the sink, sucking him with it down and down and down... He groaned as his stomach heaved; he knew that he was passing out.

*

It seemed, as consciousness passed and the threatening blackness swallowed him up, that he passed into a state which his curiously detached mind regarded as sleep. He felt no surprise at this realisation. He had often enough dreamt of sleeping before, and, doubtless, would do so again. All that concerned him now was the feeling of motion in his legs as if he was walking, though he had no idea why, or where he was going.

Some time passed by in this fashion, when he became aware of a reddish kind of glow ahead of him. Gradually it grew stronger, and he was able to make out more of his surroundings in the encrimsoned gloom: the towering trees that surrounded him with their thick, black trunks and deep morasses of leaves, rustling in the wind – the long-eared blades of grass, still wet with rain in what looked like a clearing – the surrounding blocks of weathered stone that stood like shapeless ghosts, crouching in the long grass – the glimmering red light that revealed itself to be a pile of burning wood. He

46

reached up, as if in a trance, and rubbed his eyes. Something had risen above the surging flames of the bonfire, half hidden in the smoke that billowed from it. He moved forward, feeling someone place their hands on his shoulders and force him down onto his knees. The grass felt wet through his trousers. Wet and cold. Hardly noticing this, he stared, fascinated, at the obscure shape that towered above the flames, untouched by them, his eyes deciphering what looked so much like a great, long, goat-like human head amidst the smoke. Involuntarily, Daniels looked down, away from the face that stared towards him, its yellow eyes looking straight at his with an unwavering gaze. He saw the massive cloven hoofs of the creature, restlessly pounding the earth on either side of the fire.

There was a noise in the air, like a distant chant.

*"Ma dheantar aon scriosadh..."*

Daniels looked round. A dark procession of cowled figures was advancing from a path amongst the trees, their heads bowed down towards the ground. Slowly, they gathered in huddled lines before the fire.

For a moment Daniels lost consciousness again, and there was a temporary return of the all-encompassing darkness. When it cleared, he was stunned to see that the figures had thrown off their sombre robes, their lumpy, bone-white bodies dyed red in the firelight as they knelt before it, swaying ecstatically from side to side. To his surprise Daniels recognised some of the men and women from the village amongst them. Ugly though they'd seemed when clothed, their nakedness now only served to emphasise their repulsiveness. Their rounded, almost simian shoulders were matted with patches of tangled hair, whilst their stomachs and thighs were almost black with it. Adding even more to their ugliness were other, less healthy blemishes: the running sores and deformities, their cramped, virtually toeless feet, and the coarse, almost pulpy appearance of so much of their pallid skin.

The goat-like head above the fire nodded towards them, and

Daniels caught sight of its sulphurously glowing eyes. As if this had been an expected signal, the villagers threw themselves at each other before the bonfire in complete abandon, tugging and groping and thrusting themselves at each others' bodies. It was like some wild, drug-ridden caricature of a Babylonian orgy as they writhed and twisted and groaned, sweat glistening about them as their movements became hectic, as if they were building up to some kind of joint, cumulative climax. Like a mound of swarming, discoloured worms, they rose from the ground in a seething knot of human flesh, coupling together in twos and threes and sometimes more.

Daniels frowned. Till now he had been sure it was only a dream, however disgusting it might seem. As he stared at the hideous cavorting of the villagers, though, he became suddenly aware that what he was watching was real. With each passing second he became increasingly more conscious of his surroundings and of his own physical discomfort as he knelt on the cold, wet grass.

With a cry of horror, he tried to stand up. He shook off the hands grasping at his arms and started to turn around. But, before he could see what lay hidden beneath the cowls of the two large men holding him, he saw one of them raise his arm in the air. There was a stick in his fist. It was large and heavy. The next instant he started to cry out as it crashed down at him.

*

"That's a funny kind of lump you've got on the back of your neck," Julie said suddenly, as Daniels carefully shaved himself at the fly-spotted mirror in the bathroom of the Broken Mast, his head aching as if it had been ground paper-thin with emery-cloth while he slept. "It looks like some kind of rash," she went on, sounding concerned enough for Daniels to crane his neck in the mirror to catch a glimpse of it.

"What kind of rash?" he asked, unable to see anything.

Julie stepped over to him, tying the belt of her dressing gown before reaching out one finger to feel at the rash. She

48

prodded it gingerly, curling her lip.

"I think you'd better get a doctor to have a look at it when we get to St. Auban. It looks sore. Does it hurt?"

Daniels felt at it too. His stomach almost rebelled as he moved his fingers across the lumpish crust of dried skin, perhaps two inches wide, that had formed across the nape of his neck.

"I think I will," he mumbled, his disordered recollections of the nightmare he'd had last night forgotten, as he wondered when or how this had erupted from his flesh. "It doesn't hurt, though. If you hadn't noticed it, I don't think I would have done. Not yet, anyway."

"Well, you'd better have it seen to as soon as we can. Things like that can turn nasty. It looks bad enough already." She hugged his shoulders. "I don't want anything happening to you just because you couldn't be bothered seeing a doctor."

Daniels turned and hugged her back, smiling at her, even though his head still ached with the hangover too many pints in the bar last night had left him with.

Julie combed his hair with her fingers.

"I was worried enough about you last night," she said.

"Last night?" Daniels frowned. "What happened last night?"

Julie laughed carelessly, all the worries she'd had before forgotten now.

"Don't tell me you were so drunk you can't remember where you went? You were away for more than an hour. If the landlord hadn't deigned to tell me you'd slipped outside for a breath of fresh air after being sick in the Gents, I would have been even more worried than I was. Even so, after half an hour of waiting for you in the bar, I was starting to get frantic. I thought you might have stumbled off the quay and got yourself drowned or something..."

"When did I get back?" Daniels asked, his forehead creasing with concern as he tried to remember what had happened. Surely the last thing he did was pass out in the Gents?

49

"You got back shortly after twelve, your arms over the shoulders of a couple of the locals. A dour-looking pair they were too. They said they found you sleeping near the church, propped up against the cemetery wall. You could have caught your death of cold out there on a night like that," she chided him, realising as she said it that she sounded almost like her mother. Undeterred, she went on: "You didn't even have your coat on. And your clothes were drenched. At some time or another during your rambles about the place you must have wandered off into one of the fields, because your trousers were simply covered in grass seeds. It'll be a wonder if they're not ruined."

Daniels frowned.

"It's like the nightmare I had last night," he told her. "I dreamt I was taken out into one of the fields around here, though…"

"Though what?"

"Though nothing. It was just a dream, that was all. Nothing more. Just a stupid, ridiculous, meaningless dream about some of the locals holding an open air orgy. There was a bonfire and some kind of presiding demon with a huge goat's head looking on."

"Some nightmare." Julie laughed, her joy at the fact that they would soon be leaving this place obvious as they returned to their cramped, wood-beamed bedroom to finish off their packing. Daniels glanced at the suitcases lying open on their bed, packed full of clothes. He looked past the bed and out through the tiny window that overlooked the woods at the back of the inn, where the hill sloped up from the bay. It was strange how the mere fact that they were leaving here at noon could have buoyed up his wife's spirits, while his own, if anything, were depressed. Yet he knew that he had detested their stay here just as much as she had. Perhaps more so, in fact, since he blamed himself for having picked this God-awful place to start with.

Perhaps it was because she felt well, while he felt as if he

50

was coming down with something. Serve him right if he was, he supposed, after falling asleep, pissed, in the rain. His arms and legs were aching and stiff, and he could feel a griping pain in his chest. As Julie turned her attention to packing the last items in the suitcases, Daniels again passed his fingers across the lump on his neck, hoping that the way he felt hadn't got anything to do with it.

*

After breakfast, served up by Marsh's tight-lipped wife, they decided to go out for a walk. There were another two hours to go before their bus was due, and neither of them felt like spending the time cooped up inside the claustrophobic atmosphere of the inn.

"Where shall we go?" Julie asked as they walked down the street a short while later, its cobbles covered in a sheen of water from last night's rain. Patches of blue from between the clouds were reflected in it. "We could always go for a last stroll across the cliffs," she suggested, but Daniels shook his head.

"It's still too windy for that," he objected. "Besides, it would take too long."

Aimlessly, they wandered down the street away from the bay, heading up towards the thick woodlands surrounding it. Almost automatically Daniels headed towards one of the rutted lanes that cut meanderingly through the trees, its hedges overgrown with ferns and wild flowers. Although there was no reason for him to choose any particular lane, Daniels had the disturbingly strong impression of being drawn towards this particular one. It was ridiculous, he knew, as was the ache of trepidation in his stomach as he looked along it.

Ridiculous.

Or was it?

He felt a trickle of sweat slither down the side of his face as he gazed about the lane, as if he was looking for something –

for some sign, perhaps, that would show he had been here before.

The sky glittered between the overhanging boughs of the trees, the bright green shadows of their canopying leaves giving the lane the appearance of an undersea grotto.

"For the first time this place is actually beginning to look attractive," Julie announced. There was a faint note of regret in her voice, as if she was genuinely disappointed that this should happen just as they were about to leave. Daniels made some murmured comment in reply, too preoccupied in staring round at the trees to take much notice of what she said. What was there about this place, he wondered instead, that he felt so scared of seeing? He was sure that there was something that scared him.

But what?

"Is that smoke up ahead of us?" Julie asked. She pointed to a faint grey blur above the trees, past a bend in the lane.

"I don't know." He could feel his heart pound suddenly. "Probably nothing," he said.

"Nothing?"

"I don't know." He shook his head, his mind too fogged by fears he couldn't even understand to concentrate on what she was talking about. "Some farmers, perhaps, burning rubbish."

"Or your bonfire, the one you dreamt about last night?" she joked, though the joke fell flat on his ears.

He smiled faintly in reply as they continued down the lane. What seemed fleetingly like a large, grey squirrel raced down the side of a beech tree ahead of them, then darted beneath the ferns out of sight. Dispersing through the trees like a dense sea mist blown in from the cliffs, the smoke seemed indifferent to the wind, and unhurried.

They climbed over a turnstile where a fence barred the lane from a narrower, overgrown footpath on the other side; most of its rough, stony surface was hidden beneath tufts of grass.

"Whatever's causing all that smoke can't be all that far ahead of us now," Julie said, sniffing the air as if this would tell her what she wanted to know.

Daniels glimpsed ahead of them, where the trees opened out, perhaps fifteen or so yards further on, a large, almost circular field. For a moment he thought he could also see something white, like a stone, standing tall in the grass. Suddenly, he knew that he wanted to stop, that he wanted to turn back. It was childish, he knew, and impossible. Julie was far too stubborn – too self-willed, in fact – to be fobbed off or persuaded by any half baked excuse he might think up now.

"There's your bonfire," she said, looking round at him with a peculiar mixture of triumph and curiosity on her face.

Daniels, though, had already seen it, even as she spoke. Somehow he had known that he would. He had known it all along, at the back of his mind. The smouldering shards of wood piled high in the field crackled noisily to themselves, while here and there a dull red glow glimmered amongst them, like demonic eyes peering gloomily out from the darkness of Hell.

As they left the path and picked their way into the field through the dripping ferns, he saw the odd-looking blocks of stone. They were no longer as startlingly white as they'd seemed in his dream, and he could see that their weather-pitted surfaces were covered with patches of lichens and moss. In their symmetric positioning about the field, equidistant from each other in a rough kind of circle, they looked distinctively like the kind of Druidic temples so frequently depicted in guidebooks.

"Is this *exactly* as you dreamt it?" Julie asked.

"How or why, I don't know, but yes," Daniels answered, as he ploughed his fingers through his hair, looking round himself bewildered – and a little afraid.

"Well, there's one explanation anyway," Julie said. "You *were* here last night. Perhaps you wandered down this lane. And perhaps you really did see something going on here, some rustic celebration perhaps."

"With an orgy?" he asked, incredulous. "And what about

the devil-goat? Was that here too?"

Matter-of-factly, Julie said:

"Those you must have dreamed about afterwards. After all, you *were* drunk, dear. And there's the world of difference between this," she pointed at the remains of the bonfire, "and a devil-goat."

"I thought this was fantastic enough."

"And the rest is even more fantastic," Julie insisted. "Too fantastic, in fact. And you know it."

"I suppose you're right." Damn it, of course she was right, he told himself irritably. Why was he talking such rubbish? He knew that most of what he thought he saw last night was his own imagination. What if parts of what he seemed to remember did turn out to be true? That didn't automatically mean that everything was, did it?

Daniels looked across at the stones. At one time they might have been cut into some kind of manlike shape, but that must have been a long time ago, and countless rainfalls, winds and snows had worn whatever features the ugly, Henry Moorish things might have had into virtual oblivion.

A log exploded, its overheated juices hissing and spitting like an angry cat.

"Shall we set off back to the inn now?" Julie asked.

The bonfire was slowly caving in. A smoking cinder rolled like a severed head across the wet grass, spluttering.

As they slowly turned to leave, Daniels glimpsed the top of a tousled mop of hair being whipped out of sight beneath the ferns on the far side of the path, followed immediately by the staccato splintering of twigs, which faded hurriedly into the distance.

Exchanging amused glances of perplexity, they returned to the lane past the turnstile. Something cracked in the branches overhead. As he looked up, Daniels saw a squirrel frantically leap across the lane. Its front paws grasped the outstretched branches on the other side, before disappearing amongst the leaves. It was so quiet now that sounds like those made by the frightened squirrel seemed magnified, snapping through the static air. The wind had gone now, and the overhanging veil of smoke seemed to hang, as if painted against the sky in faded water-colours.

So intense was the silence filling the lane that Daniels felt as if he could hear something faint in the distance, unreal and yet seemingly real somehow. It was probably his imagination deceiving him, he thought as they strolled down the lane. The trees obscured any sign yet of the village, and it would be at least fifteen minutes, he knew, before the first low, sunken roof would appear through the leaves.

Daniels knitted his brows as he suddenly listened with greater intensity. Surely there was something... something faint back behind them, though Julie did not seem to have heard anything.

"*Ma dheantar aon scriosadh...*" The words seemed to steal insidiously through the air. "*...gearradh lot no milleadh ar an ordu, feadfar diultu d'e a ioc...*" Daniels felt a shiver of recognition, dim and primordial.

"What's the matter?" Julie had taken him by one arm. He felt faint, and there were beads of sweat trickling down his forehead. He closed his eyes for a moment and said that he was all right, though he knew that he wasn't.

"It's nothing," he said. As he spoke he heard the vague words again.

"*...gearradh lot no milleadh ar an ordu, ar an feadfar, ar an...*"

"Can you hear something?" he asked finally, unable to hold the question back any longer.

Julie laughed, puzzled at his intense seriousness, and shook her head.

"Apart from a bee somewhere nearby, nothing," she told him. "Nothing at all. Why? Should I?"

Daniels clenched his fists as he thought again of the dream that had been haunting him all day. He caught again the far off, half heard singing.

"*...aon scriosadh, creo milleadh, ar an ordu...*"

Was it nearer?

"I can hear something," he said. "I can hear them chanting. I heard them last night when I was here. I can hear them now. I'm sure of it."

"You're imagining things," Julie insisted, dismayed at the way in which her husband's reason seemed to be disintegrating before her eyes. His face was pale and shone with perspiration as he nervously glanced back over his shoulder down the lane. What was he imagining now? she wondered. "There isn't any chanting," she insisted again, with an attempt at firmness. "It's in your mind."

He shook his head, unable to ignore the sly whispering through the trees. It was as if they were surrounded by the unseen chanters, hidden behind the undergrowth.

"Look," Julie told him, "if there was anything to hear, surely I'd be hearing it as well."

"Perhaps," Daniels said, doubtfully. Wouldn't the sounds just stop for a moment so that he could think? They seemed to slide intrusively into his mind, *into his thoughts.*

"Why won't they stop?" he shouted suddenly.

Julie tried to calm him. She looked into his eyes beseechingly, her face paling with apprehension.

"What's the matter?" she asked as he tensed, listening, though not listening to her. And for the first time, as she watched him, she could hear something too. What was it? she wondered. Someone singing? But no, that was ridiculous – *too* ridiculous!

Daniels seemed to be straining, as if he was trying to block out the words from his mind. Perspiration trickled down his forehead. His fists were knotted tight.

"*...aon scriosadh, minon a d'horga, aon e...*"

The sounds were more distinct now, nearer. There was no mistaking them. Julie felt a shiver race down her spine as she looked about herself through the surrounding trees.

"*...ma dheantar aon...*"

56

Nearer now, clearer, sibilantly piercing the stillness of the air.

"John," his wife whispered, "what's wrong? What is it?"

Daniels gritted his teeth. He turned round to face Julie.

"I don't know what it is," he said at last with an effort. "I can only tell you what I feel. And what I feel is that there's something wrong, something *horribly* wrong. There's something evil in this place. Laugh at me if you like, but that's what I feel."

"I'm not laughing," Julie replied. "There is something... something strange... something horrible. I can feel it myself now. And those sounds!" She pressed her hands against the sides of her head, as if to seal them out.

"*...ar an ordu, ar an...*"

"We've almost an hour to go before the bus arrives," Daniels said. "Somehow, I don't think we'll be there to meet it unless we can get some kind of sanctuary in the meantime. Something will happen. I know it will. The villagers – or some of them, at least – were here last night. Why, I don't know. But, in some way, I know we're involved. I'm certain. They did something to me. God knows what it was, but I'm sure it was something. I can feel it inside me." He pounded his forehead with the heel of his fist. "Something deep inside me. Deep. So very deep..."

The chants oscillated, ringing through their ears. As they hurried down the lane, it was as if the chanters followed them through the surrounding forest. Daniels tried to ignore them, but they were too loud now, too insistent. As they came at last to the edge of the village they paused. Daniels pointed to the jutting grey spire of the church.

"We'll go in there till the bus arrives. I'm sure we'll be safer in there."

The tall, dark elms cast a welcoming shadow of tranquillity about the church as they pushed open the iron gate into the grounds and hurried towards it. Daniels breathed in the purer air of the place as the chanting died into an unintelligible, insect-like drone behind them. What doubts he might still have had about the nature of whatever it was that was wrong with the village were dispersed as they experienced the spiritual peace and sense of tranquillity which the bare, stone walls of the church contained within them.

When they finally regained some of their composure, as they stood in the stone-flagged porch, looking out across the churchyard back towards the lane they had hurried along, they saw a man walk out from it, heading for the gate facing them. His heavy greatcoat hung untidily from his rounded shoulders. Even as he watched him, Daniels noticed more of the villagers making their way up the narrow, winding, cobblestone street from the quay towards the church. They seemed to be carrying heavy bundles in their arms, held tight against their chests. When they reached the gate a few moments later, Daniels realised that they were carrying bundles of wood. They tossed them on the ground by the gate, before conferring with the man and glancing now and then at the church, at the same time making peculiar signs across their chests with the tips of their fingers, as if they were somehow warding something off. Daniels frowned; more of the villagers were heading up the street. Like the first ones, these too were carrying bundles of wood.

"What are they doing?" Julie asked, apprehensively gripping tight onto his arm.

He shook his head, unable and unwilling to conjecture, to face all the fears building up inside him.

"I don't know," he said as the second batch of villagers reached the gate, casting their bundles of twigs next to the others. While most of them then returned to the village, others remained about the churchyard wall, like sentinels.

The sky was starting to darken now, as if a storm was on its way. It was appreciably colder, and they shivered as they watched the flaccid and unhealthy faces of the villagers staring at them from above the rough, stone walls about the church. The leaden sky seemed to match the pasty, grey pallor of their flesh.

Daniels glanced at his watch.

"The bus will be due any time now," he said. "Shall we make a break for it?"

There was no choice. If they missed the bus they would be stuck here till tomorrow. His left arm about Julie's shoulders, Daniels pushed the door open and they stepped out. As they did so, the villager stood guard at the gate brought out a pick handle, clenched with both hands.

Julie pressed back, frightened, against her husband's chest.

"We'll never make it," she whispered.

Grunting something, Daniels led them back through the porch into the church.

"It's obvious what those bastards want to do," he grunted, trying to fight back his fears. "We can't stay here indefinitely, yet they won't let us leave."

"What do they want of us? Why are they trying to keep us here?" Julie asked, close to tears as she peered through the open doorway, back across the path through the churchyard to the gate, where the man stood waiting, staring back at them with a cold, unwavering gaze.

Daniels remembered his dream last night, and he knew that he could not reply. The villagers had always struck him as degenerate, unhealthily so, but there was much more wrong with them than that, something far worse than the excesses of inbreeding. He thought of the cheesy, hair-covered bodies he saw cavorting before the bonfire last night. He realised just how grotesquely similar they were, in a hybridly abortive way, to the demonic goat above the fire, with their excessively hairy legs and satyr-like faces, their yellow eyes burning with unholy and hideous lusts. Although he had never been a deeply religious man, he had no doubts now but that what he saw above the fire was the incarnation of a devil, of the goat-headed spirit of some Hellish and damnable satyr. He shuddered with revulsion. So far the villagers had made no attempt to communicate with them. It was as if they had no real use for speech and were indifferent to it. Had they degenerated so far, he wondered as he watched more of them silently making their way to the churchyard wall, that they were now little better than beasts?

The sky had darkened considerably, almost as if the sun had sunk beneath the hills and the blackness of night was gathering about the sheltered village. There was a feeling of expectancy in the air, an electrical, tingling lull.

In the murky light the villagers seemed to coalesce into a single, indistinguishable mass. As he peered at them he thought he saw the brief flare of a match. A moment later, in confirmation, flames began to flicker in the gloom. The crackling of burning wood broke through the silence, and a cloud of smoke rose into the air. More flames appeared from about the churchyard walls. Daniels realised that they must have set fire to the bundles of twigs. But why? Did they intend to try and smoke them out of the church?

The flames grew brighter. Suddenly the bundles of twigs were hoisted into the air, and Daniels saw that they were being held aloft on pitchforks by the villagers. A moment later they started to scramble over the walls, pushing through the trees towards the church. Daniels slammed the heavy oak doors shut, pressing his shoulders against them.

"They're going to try and burn the church down," he cried out. An instant later there was a crash as glass was shattered in one of the tall, stained-glass windows, and one of the bundles flared through it, multicoloured fragments of glass cascading down amidst the flames. Sparks erupted fiercely over the pews underneath like incandescent waves of lava as more bundles were thrust through the windows. Daniels knew that the wood must have been soaked in petrol or some other highly flammable liquid. Thick clouds of smoke billowed out, filling the church with an acrid, unbreathable stench of burning. Daniels saw one of the pews ignite as flames spread like a darkening, blood-red, iridescent stain across it.

"We've got to get out of here," Julie screamed. Wild-eyed,

she scanned the smoke-filled, flame-ripped shambles of the church as more bundles of sticks were thrust through the windows.

Daniels took her by one arm and said:

"When I open the door we'll make a dash for it. Maybe – just maybe – they'll not see us in the smoke. But stick close to me. We mustn't get separated in the confusion." He reached for one of the half burnt bundles of wood and tore out enough to form a heavy torch. Then, with one last pat of reassurance on his wife's shoulders, he flung the doors open. A villager was waiting outside. A look of devilish satisfaction lit the man's face, his thick, almost Negroid lips curling back from his teeth as his fists tightened about the heavy stick he was holding like a club. The next instant his mouth was contorted with agony as Daniels thrust the smouldering end of his torch into his eyes. There was a hideous scream, and the man reeled uncontrollably backwards, clutching at his face. Daniels kicked him hard in the kidneys as he went down, then turned to pull Julie after him as they ran across the churchyard for the wall. He could hear the chanting again now, but it wasn't clear. Smoke obscured everything, and with this and the glowering darkness of the sky, it was difficult to see. Savage blades of fire were mercilessly cutting through the church roof now as if through an enormous cardboard model, and it would not be long before it was a raging, self-consuming inferno. His only hope was that the bulk of the villagers would think that they were still trapped inside.

There was a rumbling of thunder, which seemed to reverberate through the ground as if from deep beneath the earth. It was difficult for Daniels to believe that it was still midday, so dark was the sky. Any moment he expected a sudden downpour of rain to drench them.

"Which way is it to where the bus comes in?" Julie asked as they scrambled over the churchyard wall, its old stones crumbling beneath their fingers. Skidding on the cobbles underneath, they ran down the street into the village. Daniels

61

looked at his watch. Was there still time to reach it? he wondered frantically.

"That way, I think," he stammered, indicating a narrow street that curved off to their left between rows of tiny, tumble-down cottages, their walls all but hidden by mats of climbers.

Somewhere he heard what sounded like a horse galloping across the cobbles. Thunder rumbled yet again, deep and sonorous, echoing through the wooded slopes of the valley. The hoof-beats came again. Nearer this time.

"Run!" Daniels cried as he tugged at his wife. "Run!"

Something loomed ahead of them through the smoke. It was the back of the single-decker bus, its rear lights piercing the gloom as it started up. Together they made a dash for it, but it was already driving away from them.

"Wait!" Daniels shouted as the gap lengthened between them. Its shadow merged into the smoke as it trundled round a bend in the street. Tree boughs reached out from the hedgerow as the smoke dispersed on the outskirts of the village. "Stop!" Daniels shouted, but he knew that it was too late. They couldn't hear him. The bus was already going out of sight. It gathered speed as the driver changed gears up the hill.

"*...ma dheantar aon scriosadh...*"

The chanting seemed to surround them suddenly. There was a further clattering of hoofs, that echoed deafeningly through the village.

A dim figure shuffled towards them. It was the man who had spoken to them the night before. His insalubrious features shone with sweat like the belly of a long dead fish, white and puffy.

"'E's claimed you," the man said, and he pointed at Daniels. "'Is mark 'as been laid on your flesh an' you are 'Is. Don't fight against 'Im. Don't try to lock 'Im out."

"You're mad," Daniels growled. "You're all mad. Every last one of you. God knows what insane sickness has corrupted this village, but it must've rotted away what little

62

sense you had left. No one, no *thing* has laid its mark on me."

The man laughed quietly, still slowly stumbling towards them, his baggy trousers singed and tattered, his unfastened overcoat hanging from his bony shoulders as if it was several sizes too large.

"'Is mark is there," he replied, unconcerned by Daniels' denial. He placed one of his blackened, diseased-looking fingers at the back of his neck. "'Is mark is there. Where it can grow," he went on ominously. "Where it can grow."

Julie gasped something beside him. What was it she whispered? The lump? *The lump!*

"NNNOOO!" Daniels cried, hurling the torch in desperation at the man, as if to block out his words.

There was a further clattering of hoofs. They were near, now, only just out of sight, he was sure.

Daniels turned round to Julie.

"We'll get out of here even if we have to run all the way to St. Auban."

"You defy 'Im uselessly," the villager called out mockingly as they ran along the lane in the same direction in which the bus had gone only minutes before.

"...*gearradh lot no milleadh ar an ordu, ar an feadfar...*"

The black storm clouds were boiling up from the horizon in even thicker, even denser formations, till they smothered the sun. As the light faded, so the chanting seemed to grow still louder, so the hoof-beats seemed to spread still further and further from the church, into the village and countryside.

As they ran, Daniels felt the chants slide into his mind, blocking his thoughts. He shook his head. In front of them he seemed to see something tall and black watching them. When he concentrated on looking at it, though, he saw that it was nothing more than an old, dead tree.

*Why did he keep thinking that he must stop and return to the village? Rites? There were no rites for him to perform. The tree. Yes, it was there again. It was only a tree. Why did he imagine that it was something else? Ridiculous! Keep*

*running. Can't let them catch up.*
  *MUST PERFORM RITES, THOUGH. MUST!*
  *WHAT RITES?*
Daniels tried to keep his thoughts straight, but ideas and impressions kept assailing him.
  *WHAT RITES DID HE KEEP THINKING ABOUT?*
His fingers clenched as if to take hold of a knife. Realising what he was doing, he opened them. He felt sweat bead his face. He strained against the alien thoughts and urges that were infiltrating his mind as he stared ahead of them.
  *There was that figure again. Black goat's legs. Hoof-beats. No, there was nothing there. A shadow. That was all. Just a shadow!*
With increasing difficulty they hurried up the lane. The smoke followed them implacably. The sly, insidious and piercing chants continued to pursue them, as if they were stalking them like some sort of prey. Black goat images continued to flash through his mind. Again and again. He remembered the dream.
  *No, that was rubbish. RUBBISH!*
It came over him suddenly. For an instant he felt short of breath, and he wondered if he was about to collapse. The hoof-beats returned. They seemed to clatter within his head, hammering his thoughts into oblivion. He caught hold of Julie's arm and swung her round in front of him. The smoke closed in. As Julie screamed uncomprehendingly, he felt something cold being pressed into his hand. With instinctive rapidity he raised it. Something hot and wet gushed across his hand. He heard a scream. It was far, so far away, lost as if through vast and echoing caverns. He saw Julie's face turn grey before him like a *papier mache* mask. Her mouth opened, slowly, straining the muscles in her cheeks. Something red blossomed out of it, slithering towards him, splashing his face as he moved his hand further. There was a resistance. He looked down and saw the thick red blood that oozed across his hand and about the hilt of the knife that was

tightly clenched in it, jammed against the base of his wife's ribcage through her clothes. A goat-like human head, etched with a look of demonic triumph, superimposed itself in front of his eyes, as he forced the knife up till it cracked through her ribcage and she fell against him. The chanting grew into a crescendo of sound.

"*...ma dheantar aon scriosadh...*"

Blood dripped onto the ground. The sky became black. Boiled. Lightning crashed across the heavens. Ahead of him, over the sinking shoulders of his wife, Daniels saw the satyr watching him, its arms folded across its chest, its goat's mouth gaping as its long, red tongue slid sensuously across its teeth.

He looked round. The villagers, their degenerate features alight with an unhealthy semblance of joy, emerged from the smoke. He knew that he was one of them now.

Now and forever more...

# THE COLD HARVEST

## Steve Goodwin

"Eeh... I'd like to cut thy 'ead off."

Old Mrs Siddall standing by the gate, sharpening her knife –
as she always is when I walk past her, on the other side of the
road, on my way to school. I'm afraid of Old Mrs Siddall but if
I walk the other way, down the back lane, I have to pass the
Jennings Farm where the dog always runs out snarling and
tries to bite me – and did once, taking a big piece out of my
new coat. They ought to keep the bloody thing chained up, my
dad says. So I always walk the long way round, past the chapel
and the pub opposite, over the canal, follow the park wall up to
the church, cross the road and past Mrs Siddall's house.

Mrs Siddall lives alone now and only the Reverend Turner
ever goes to the house. She must be very lonely. When the old
lady was younger, my mum told me, she lived in the house
with her father and her two brothers and they used to drink and
fight all the time. Mrs Siddall would be in the kitchen cooking
the dinner for when the men came home from work, and she'd
get everything ready and lay the table and then they'd come in
drunk and start shouting and cursing. Once the younger brother
was standing at the stove sniffing at the stew that she'd made
and the older brother came up behind him and shouted;
"Tonight you die, you bugger... die!" and pushed the younger
brother's head into the pan and held it there. And then when
he'd let go, the younger brother came up spluttering all scalded
and covered in stew and grabbed the big bread knife and
chased the older brother round the garden. I thought it sounded
funny when my mum told me that but it can't have been very
nice for the old lady, living in a house where that kind of thing
happened all the time.

So, when I walk past her every morning and she's there,
sharpening her knife and telling me how much she'd like to cut
my head off, I try not to look at her and I'm scared in case she

66

comes running after me, like the dog, but she never does and I
suppose I feel sorry for her. For everything she had to put up
with and for what happened to her baby.

This morning, by the church, I meet Mr Jennings coming up
from the lich field with half a fresh lich slung over his
shoulder, taking it up to the farm. He smiles and says, "Lovely
morning for it," and walks by and I try and smile but the smell
from the lich is awful so I run on to school as fast as I can.
They say it's been another bad year for Mr Jennings and the
other farmers in the village – the crops still aren't growing and
the animals won't breed. Things have never been right again
since The Pest, and that was nearly twenty years ago before I
was born.

After school, I stop by the church. I always stop somewhere
on my way home. Sometimes on the little bridge over the canal
and watch the barges passing by – I often think about jumping
off the bridge when a barge is passing underneath and landing
on the deck or the brightly painted roof and letting it carry me
away to the city. Or the sea. Sometimes I stop off at The Vine
to see Uncle Abel, who's always sitting outside putting the
world to rights with his friends. Uncle Abel likes to drink at
The Vine – I've heard he has his post delivered there now – so
that he can heckle the Methodists as they're coming out of
chapel. Bloody 'eathens he calls them. Worse than the Tories,
he says, and he hates them so much that once, when the man
next door voted for the Tories, Uncle Abel painted his cat
blue. Uncle Abel is a Liberal. I thought that was funny too, but
my mum said it was cruel. Poor cat. I don't think Uncle Abel
meant to hurt the cat and I'm sure that it was an accident when
he killed it last year. Abel was digging in his garden and the
cat came through the fence and started scratching at his
marrows – and marrows were the only thing he'd been able to
grow since The Pest – so Abel threw his spade at the cat, just
to scare it away he says, but the spade hit the cat and killed it.
Cut it clean in half, Abel says, he bets he couldn't do it again if
he tried. Uncle Abel likes betting too. Anyway, he thought the

man next door would never believe it was an accident, what with him having painted the cat the year before, so he just buried it in the garden and said nothing. Mum thinks the man next door knows; "'E wouldn't just 'ave wandered off and not come back. 'E's a very loyal cat," he said. "What does thee expect from a Tory cat?" Abel told him, "Thee can never trust a Tory."

I like spending time with my Uncle Abel after school because he lets me have sips of his beer and a puff on his pipe and he's funny with the Methodists. Yesterday one of them came over when he saw me drinking beer and called me a 'poor child' and said that Abel should be ashamed of himself. And when my uncle stood up to go and get himself another drink, Mr Pennington, the Methodist, stood in his way and started shouting about how beer is 'the devil's brew' and how Abel shouldn't be smoking because his body is a temple. And Abel was trying to get past but Mr Pennington kept walking backwards in front of him, all the way to the door of the pub, and shouting up into my uncle's face; "If the good Lord had meant us to smoke, he'd have given us chimneys in the tops of our heads!"

"Aye," said Abel, "and if the good Lord 'ad meant us to walk backwards, he'd 'ave given us eyes in our arses. Now bugger off out of the way!"

And Mr Pennington saw me laughing and scowled at me and then buggered off, muttering all the time under his breath about us being 'sinners'.

But today I decide that I won't stop off at the pub and see Uncle Abel, or stand on the bridge and watch the barges, I'll go to the church and see all those people that died from The Pest.

I don't really like thinking about death. I don't like thinking about death and I don't really like dead things either, but the Reverend Turner says that there is a season for everything. A time to be born and a time to die. A time to sow and a time to reap. It's the way of all things and it says so in The Bible. And when some people said that was as may be but it still didn't seem right to them – about the liches – the Reverend Turner told them to read in Genesis where it says, 'every moving thing that lives shall be meat to you', and in First Corinthians where it's written, 'Whatsoever is sold in the meat-markets, that eat, asking no question for conscience sake: For the earth is the Lord's, and the fullness thereof.' And their souls are up in heaven not down here on the earth, he said, and it was wrong to let a lich rot away when it could be buried in the field where the cold ground would keep it fresh until it was needed.

Reverend Turner came to Dunham the year after The Pest.

It froze last night, and this morning when I got up the earth was hard with frost and a thin covering of snow was spread out across the empty fields. It'll soon be Christmas.

Mrs Siddall was old when she married. Forty-one, my mother says. I heard her talking to Auntie Davies from next door one day when I was playing in the yard. Mrs Siddall's young man came from one of the nearby villages and had been calling on her for some time in spite of her father and her two brothers. The first time he visited the house he'd left his bicycle outside and the older brother took it and rode it to the pub and sold it. But the young man still came back.

Finally, her father gave them permission to get married. Everyone was surprised, mum said, because things had happened in that house that shouldn't ought to happen in any family, but anyway the young man and Mrs Siddall were married and lived together in the house with the father and brothers. Some people say that the reason she was allowed to marry her sweetheart was because she had a baby on the way. And mum says it's true that not more than six months after the wedding, Mrs Siddall gave birth to a little boy. But she says, it's a funny thing, because she'd heard that Mrs Siddall had told the midwife that she knew what people were saying about her and the young man but it wasn't true, none of it, and she swore that there'd been no funny business before the wedding.

It's very sad the baby died. The winter was very bad that year, even worse than usual. Nobody had enough food to eat, so what chance did a little baby have? Mum remembers the morning it happened. Mrs Siddall was out in the back garden, screaming and crying her eyes out, saying how it was all wrong and these things shouldn't be allowed to happen, and she didn't give a damn what the minister had to say about it, she just wanted her baby back. And her father came outside in his shirt and his braces hanging down and shouted at her not to be so bloody stupid and get back inside.

Mrs Siddall lost her husband that same winter.

The Pest killed over half of all the people in the village, but it was worse for those that survived they say, because it also killed almost all the livestock and folk were near dying of hunger. And nothing grew in the fields. Everyone turned to the pastor at the church and asked why God had let this happen and what was he going to do about it. The pastor told them not to lose faith and God would show them the way, but a few months later he just left one night without telling anyone he was going. That's when the Reverend Turner came.

The Reverend Turner is a very tall man with funny eyes, and when he talks you have to listen. There's something about his voice that makes you believe what he says is right and true. He called everyone into the church that first day and they all came, even the Methodists. He told them that they were foolish, that their suffering was needless because the Lord would always provide. People were still dying every day, not from The Pest but from the hunger. Children and old people mostly. It was clear what had to be done, he said, if we didn't want the whole village to die. The Methodists said it was the Devil's work, that he was tempting us and they'd have no part of it. Help would come from the other villages eventually if people would just bear the suffering and stay faithful to God. The Reverend Turner said that he'd been to all the villages nearby and things

70

were no different there. No help would ever come from the outside. We were alone and must provide for our families in the only way we could.

That was how Reverend Turner saved the village.

Things have got better in the years since then. In my lifetime. But we still wouldn't have enough to eat without the liches. I don't really like it, and I tried telling my mum once that I'd rather just have the marrows that Uncle Abel gave us from his garden. She got very cross and dad told me I was an ungrateful little bugger and that I ought to be thankful we'd got any food on the table at all. I think the thing that worries me most is that people aren't dying as often as they were in the old days and I don't see how they keep the lich field stocked. Nobody ever talks about that.

When I saw Mrs Siddall on my way to school this morning, I thought perhaps I should try talking to her. She didn't really look like she wanted to talk to me though, she just kept staring at me. It was even queerer than normal. It's very cold again today and my coat's not as warm as it was since the Jennings' dog put a hole in it, even though mum tried to mend it as best she could. I was early so I stopped on the bridge for a bit. No barges today. They don't come as often as they used to. I suppose things are difficult everywhere. I can see all the fields from the bridge and they're mostly bare. There's a little hill in one of the fields, that everyone calls Weepy Will. I'm not sure why. I think that it might be an old burial mound like we learned about in History, not from the time of The Pest, much older than that. When I'm older I'd like to go digging there to see if there's any treasure. If I found some treasure, even a little bit, I could get away from the village and go wherever I liked and eat whatever I wanted.

I couldn't sleep last night. I'm not really looking forward to Christmas this year. It's not like it used to be when I was little.

I think it's because I'm old enough to know now that a lot of the things that my mum and dad told me, aren't really true. I lay awake, shivering under my blanket because it was so cold, and I could hear the grown-ups talking downstairs. They were arguing about something, my mum and dad, and Uncle Abel had come round and I'm sure I heard the Reverend Turner's voice. It must have been something very important. Something serious. Mum was crying and dad kept swearing and then apologising to Reverend Turner. Uncle Abel was saying that he wouldn't stand for it, whatever it was. He was swearing too but he never apologised. Then he went out and slammed the door behind him. I heard Reverend Turner ask if it was settled then, if they'd definitely decided. My mum didn't say anything, but my dad said yes, they'd made their decision and they were going to abide by it. Then I could hear my dad and the Reverend Turner talking on the doorstep for a bit and, just before he went, Reverend Turner said well, if they were sure he'd have a word with Mrs Siddall in the morning.

# ALL UNDER HATCHES STOW'D

## Mike Chinn

She was standing on the water's edge, listening for something – but she didn't remember what. Behind her, the jungle breathed and sighed. She smelled its rank heat; felt a tickle as something warm ran from her nose. It was so calm and peaceful – and then she heard the scream.

Yukashi jerked awake, a shriek of her own building in her throat. Three shots reverberated from outside, barely dulled by her cabin window: evenly spaced, quite deliberate – but no more screams. She dropped back on her bed and took several deep breaths – it was probably De Broek. Again.

It was always De Broek.

Once her heart had slowed enough, she got out of bed and grabbed for the nearest thing she had to a robe: her stained lab coat. Pulling it on, she slammed out of her meagre quarters, ran up the nearest steps and onto the deck. The sky was pale violet with the promise of a sun still two hours away. Clearly silhouetted against the lightening sky was De Broek – the stock of his vintage Mauser rifle still butted against his shoulder – standing against a rail, watching the water carefully.

"Three in a boat," he said – though Yukashi could have sworn he didn't know she was there. "Got 'em all." His flat, South African accent turned the plain statement into something more sinister.

She joined him at the rail. The water was as lurid as the sky, and she could easily make out a small boat, empty and drifting around twenty metres away. Apart from the ripples off the boat's hull, the lake was calm. Beyond, the jungle was a solid, undulating black mass – unusually silent, after the gunshots.

"Were they infected?" she asked.

De Broek shrugged. "How the hell should I know?"

"You could have waited—"

"*Fok jou!*" He turned on her angrily. Even though he was

73

only five feet tall – no taller than Yukashi – she still felt like he towered over her. "You think I'm going to wait? *Kak!*" He spun away again before she could respond.

Yukashi wanted to be able to say something – to throw some unassailable humanitarian argument in his ugly face – but she knew there wasn't one. Just because there was no sign of the disease didn't mean they weren't infected; and if they got close enough for you to see the symptoms, you were dead.

*

Yukashi was probably the first one to witness it. She was supervising the day's logging operation – watching the workmen with a concern that they never demonstrated. Every few minutes some idiot would saunter blithely in front of a machine that could fell and strip a tree in seconds. Yukashi didn't like to think what one would do to a man. Burrell was in his cab one second – his logger in front as usual, slicing through the rainforest like a rat through balsa – the next, he was gone.

Yukashi started running towards the still active logger, her fear about what an unpiloted machine could do drowning any thought of Burrell. Not until she'd vaulted into the cab and turned off the ignition did she stop and wonder about him. By then, several of the logging team had caught up, and were huddled on the ground; about ten metres back from the logger's rear axle.

*Shit!* thought Yukashi – *don't tell me he got run over!*

She dropped to the ground and strode towards the group. They parted reluctantly – she was only a woman, and at least a foot shorter than any of the men. At the focus of the huddle was Burrell, lying in a knot on the hard ground. His black face looked darker than ever – but that could have been the sweat trickling off him – and thin dribbles of blood were coming from his mouth and nose. Yukashi thought he might be moaning, but couldn't tell over the babble of voices. They sounded more angry then concerned, she thought – but they always sounded angry to her. Like her father, when he slipped into the harsh Japanese she'd never learned.

"Back off for Christ's sake!" she shouted, waving at them with her clipboard. They shuffled back a little, their voices dropping enough for Yukashi to hear Burrell's groaning. The blood seemed to be flowing more heavily from his mouth. Internal damage, she guessed. The ground was covered with stumps no more than a foot high; if he'd fallen across one of those he could have broken his back, easy. For a moment she thought he was getting louder – then she realised all the other loggers had been turned off, the crews coming to see what the excitement was.

Yukashi unhooked the transceiver from her belt. "De Broek? You there?"

For ten seconds all she got back was static that set her teeth on edge. Then De Broek's flat voice cut through the noise.

"I'm here. Who's that?"

"Yukashi. I'm out on the north shore. We've got a man down. It could be serious – I think we'll need a chopper."

"*Kak!*" The static washed over his voice for an instant. "Who is it?"

*Does it matter?* Yukashi wondered. "Burrell Makelele. He's a gang leader—"

"I know who he is. What the stupid *kaffir* do – cut a leg off...?"

"No – he fell from his cab, hit the floor. He seems to be bleeding in—"

"Fell from the cab!" The static swarmed back in; for a moment, Yukashi thought De Broek had cut her off.

"—kay, I'll radio for a chopper." His voice cut back in abruptly. "Keep an eye on him – make sure he doesn't start to choke, or something... And keep the other *kaffirs* away – they'll steal his teeth, given the chance..."

The static cut back in, signalling he was gone properly this time. Yukashi toggled frequencies. "Mr Adjatay? Do you copy? Mr Adjatay…?"

She waited about twenty seconds, and was about to call again when Edmund Adjatay's voice answered her. "Adjatay here. What's the trouble?"

"This is Yukashi, Mr Adjatay. On the north-east shore. We have a man down—"

Adjatay interrupted smoothly. When he wasn't angry he did everything smoothly – like stabbing someone with a warmed stiletto. "I'm sorry, Miss Matsuda – but why is this my concern…?"

"It's a safety issue, Mr Adjatay – I have to report all—"

"Then consider it reported, Miss Matsuda. Replace him and continue the felling."

"But, Mr Adjatay—"

"Thank you. Adjatay out…"

The transceiver went utterly quiet. No interference on Edmund Adjatay's frequency; it wouldn't dare. Yukashi gave a quiet shriek and allowed the transceiver to hang from its strap.

She bent over Burrell. The blood was definitely flowing more heavily from his mouth – maybe even his nose. She could see De Broek's point. But Burrell appeared to be breathing easily – and his groans were loud enough. Most of the other workmen had gone back to their loggers – excitement over for the day. Above the over-revving of the machines' huge diesel engines, she could hear the thud of an approaching chopper.

"You'll be okay, Burrell," she said, calmly as she could. "Be in hospital soon…"

\*

But he hadn't made it that far. Burrell was pronounced DOA, and although Yukashi hadn't heard the full details – there'd been little time in the end, and details were the first thing to get lost – she guessed it had been pretty horrific. Lots of bleeding – and not just internal haemorrhaging: eyes, ears – even skin pores. The fall had been the least of his problems. After that, it just became a nightmare. Two of the paramedics from the chopper died within six hours – same symptoms as Burrell, far as Yukashi could tell. Then hospital staff began to get sick. All contact was lost twenty-fours after Burrell had died, but neither Yukashi, De Broek, or any of the others had needed what must have happened spelling out. Burrell had picked up some disease that killed within hours. Everyone at the hospital was presumed dead.

Which left two questions: did anyone else have it? And just where had Burrell been infected?

As soon as the hospital had fallen silent, all the local workers had vanished. Assuming the site was infected, or cursed, or whatever. Yukashi's worst fear had been that one or more of them were already infected. She had no data: with the hospital gone, and only the most obvious symptoms to go on, there was nothing but very poor guesswork left. She had no idea when it became infectious – before the symptoms manifested or after? And was it transmitted through the air, or did it need contact?

\*

Adjatay was screaming down the radio again. Whoever was at the receiving end wasn't giving in easily – a personality trait Edmund Adjatay never appreciated. But no matter how much he threatened, cajoled, bullied or bribed, the result was the same: no planes could land anywhere near Lake Tego, and there were no choppers available. Adjatay and his stranded group of loggers would have to sit it out.

Which translated as: we're not risking some unknown disease just to haul out a bunch of illegal tree-fellers.

Adjatay threw the mike at the radio and turned to glower at everyone in the cabin – daring anyone to speak. Begging, almost.

*Maybe he should have tried begging over the radio,*

Yukashi thought.

"Go ahead – break the radio," De Broek murmured, not bothering to look up from the leather sofa he was sprawled across. Like every other object in the room, it was a co-ordinated white. "That'll solve everything."

Adjatay surged towards the small South African – an immaculate tower of fury. His dark olive skin was slick and pale, mixed racial features twisted. His bleached cotton shirt clung to him in damp patches. For a moment, it looked as though he was actually going to seize De Broek – his hands were snatching at the air like hungry talons; then he spun away and slammed out of the cabin.

"Prick," muttered De Broek, settling himself deeper into the sofa.

"If anyone wants me, I'll be in my room…" The speaker erupted into deep laughter that Yukashi imagined vibrating throughout the cabin. It was Pascal Bokhani, or course – the only one left on board the *Busiris* who could laugh any more. The giant Malian was incapable of taking anything seriously – not Adjatay's furious ego, De Broek's posturing; not even her own lurking paranoia.

"A hundred bucks he's going to spend all night sulking with his films," muttered De Broek.

"No," replied Bokhani. "*One* film."

"Not even Adjatay can spend all night watching just one movie!" De Broek objected, swinging himself into a sitting position.

"One film," insisted Bokhani. As usual, he looked as though he was about to burst out laughing at some private joke. But it wasn't so private – all three of them knew which of Adjatay's hundreds of DVDs he spent most time watching.

"*Prospero's Books*," Yukashi said to herself. She'd sat through it once – at Adjatay's insistence – and it had been a trial. Even the threat of her boss's unpredictable anger hadn't been quite enough to keep her watching. In the end, she'd stayed just to find out what was so fascinating. And she hadn't

seen it: some exiled magician's chance for revenge against his
enemies simply vanishes when his daughter and his enemy's
son fall in love. Didn't seem Adjatay's kind of thing –
especially as the old British actor playing the magician was the
only one who spoke. Everything else was music and dancing.

Afterwards he'd raped her, of course. As she'd struggled,
and he'd beaten her into submission, Adjatay had kept up a
quiet murmuring – talking to himself. It wasn't until the last
moments, as he brutally climaxed and the murmurs became
shouts, that she made out the words.

"'*As you from crimes would pardon'd be, Let your
indulgence set me free!*'"

*

Yukashi lurched out of another nightmare. Even though her
tiny cabin was barely above freezing, sweat sheathed her like a
second, oily skin. Whatever the dream had been about, it was
already fragmenting – the harder she tried to remember it, the
faster it fled. All she recalled was the fear, and a sense of
claustrophobia – and the red. Always red.

Yukashi got out of bed and dragged off her damp pyjamas.
Pulling on a tracksuit top and bottoms, she left the cabin,
pushing lank strands of hair from her eyes. She wanted a drink
of water – but somehow found herself in the lab, instead. There
was nothing to drink here – unless she wanted to risk the
absolute ethanol. Pure alcohol – not a trace of contaminant.
She wondered how much she'd be able to swallow before it
killed her.

She flicked on the lights, and cold fluorescent tubes strobed
into life. The lab was drowned in hard, clinical light that
allowed few shadows. Yukashi crossed her arms – starting to
shiver, now – and stared at the well-stocked shelves, the two
benches, balances, microscope, UV scanner and computer...
Clean and antiseptic, top of the range – and useless. For all the
compounds and solutions and polished glassware, there wasn't

a thing she could do about whatever was killing everyone outside. Even if she could get a sample of blood or tissue – and survive long enough to process it – there were no tests she could perform. The lab was just another of Adjatay's expensive toys – an environmental sop to his company. To collect and study all the species they might encounter – just before destroying their habitat drove them to extinction.

Yukashi shrieked. With a single sweep of her right arm she shattered beakers and flasks, spilled pretty fluids over the computer, sent the microscope rolling to the floor. Her nose and throat were pricked by the astringent smell of mixing and evaporating flammables – and for a moment she toyed with the idea of a lighted match.

Instead, she slammed from the room and went to find Adjatay.

De Broek and Bokhani had been right. He was in his viewing room, spread across the wide sofa that was the only item of furniture in the room. Almost everything in the room was black: carpeting that spread up from the floor to cover walls and ceiling, the sofa itself. The only relief were the ranks of DVD boxes along one wall, Adjatay's white clothing, and the two metre-wide plasma screen at which he was staring. Sure enough, he was watching *Prospero's Books*.

Yukashi tried to slam the door behind her, but its sprung hinges resisted, and it closed noiselessly. She tried not to remember what had happened the last time she'd been down here.

"Mr Adjatay."

He didn't turn, or move at all. Yukashi raised her voice.

"Mr Adjatay!"

His head rotated gently on a neck that seemed to have grown rigid. He stared at her for several seconds; his face twitched as though he no longer remembered how to use its muscles. Or it could have been light from the screen.

"'Canst thou remember a time before we came unto this cell?'" he said eventually – his voice thin and baffled. "'I do

80

not think thou canst—'"

"Mr Adjatay – we've got to get away from here! Lake Tego should act as a natural barrier – if we moved the *Busiris* to the western shore, I'm sure—"

"No." Even though he spoke quietly – his voice barely loud enough to be heard above the film – it had enough authority to silence her. "We go nowhere."

"We're accomplishing nothing here! We're just hiding…!"

Adjatay stood up, slowly – as though every joint in his body hurt. "We are riding out the storm, Miss Matsuda." He began moving towards her, each step careful, slow. "It's like a bush fire, you see? It burns what it can and moves on. If we move across the lake, we'll be putting ourselves straight back in its path."

"It doesn't work like that!" she yelled at him – almost directly in his face. "This is a plague! The origins are still in the jungle! We unleashed it – it's not going to go away—!"

"We are not moving!" His hands seized her shoulders with a speed that was remarkable after his previous lethargy. "Do you understand?"

"Mr Adjatay—!"

*"Do you understand?"*

Yukashi collapsed against him – she couldn't fight any longer. She was too small, too weak. As her father had always reminded her – she was just a woman. Sobbing her terror out, she was oblivious as Adjatay gently hugged her, stroked her lank hair and kissed her forehead. "'I have done nothing but in care of thee,'" he murmured. "'Of thee, my dear one.'"

Eventually, the tears stopped. Yukashi rubbed at her wet face, but Adjatay still held her.

"Please, Mr Adjatay," she said, her voice harsh and cracked, "can't we go? Can't we get out of here?"

"There's no place to go," he said, his voice a tremulous whisper. Yukashi looked at him – looked closely. The lines in his face had become gaunt scars, and his eyes were hooded – retreated into their sockets.

Gently – but still remorselessly – he lowered her onto the black sofa. "'Lie there, my art,'" he whispered. "'Wipe thou thine eyes; have comfort.'"

And this time, when he took her, Yukashi didn't fight. Even the pain was some kind of reassurance.

\*

De Broek and Bokhani were both up on deck. From the amount of noise they were making, Yukashi guessed they were both drunk. It was as good a way of passing time as any.

She went up to join them. They were shouting and singing – one in Afrikaans, the other French. A huge CD player was beating out rap as a strange counterpoint to their voices. They were kicking what looked like a football about. The way it rolled erratically across the deck, along with their own unbalanced lurching, made her wonder how all three hadn't pitched into the lake before now.

De Broek spotted her and yelled out. "It's Adjatay's *hoer*! His little pet *aap*! Didn't realise you liked it rough…!"

Bokhani's booming laugh drowned the CD player for a moment. "She was so pissed off when he raped her the first time, she went back and raped him in revenge!"

Both men laughed crudely, and went back to kicking the improvised football again. Yukashi ignored them and stepped towards the boat's rail. The jungle appeared larger, somehow; she knew it couldn't be nearer: the *Busiris*'s anchor was too firm. The trees were grabbing for the steel sky with jagged, bleached fingers; vines and creepers knotted the trunks and branches with sinewy ropes that looked rank and putrid; in the shadows, she was sure she could make out things moving – but what animals would stay around and listen to De Broek and Bokhani's singing?

Something cracked against her ankle. She glanced down, even as her heart spasmed; threatening to stop altogether. It was the football – except it wasn't. A monkey's head – bloody,

82

eyeless and shedding fur and skin.

Yukashi flinched and jerked her foot back. The head rolled past the rail and into the lake.

"Thanks a lot, you stupid bint!" De Broek was at her shoulder; she turned in fright and stared straight into his furious eyes. "Where are we going to get another one, eh?"

"Where did you get that?" she asked.

"Out of the lake," Bokhani replied, for the angry South African. "Or maybe you think De Broek swam up to the jungle for it?" He laughed again – but there was something false about the sound. Something hollow. De Broek joined in.

"Yeah. That's right. I needed a dip – been cooped up on this tub without a decent soak too long..."

Yukashi was looking over the side, oblivious to them. She'd never considered anything floating across the lake. Stupid, stupid! If the crocs didn't take it, any corpse will float for a while. And if dead monkeys drifted up to the boat...

Yukashi swung back to De Broek, in her sudden fear and anger forgetting she was scared of him. "What if it carried the plague!" she screamed, almost in his face. "Did you bother to think about that?"

"If it affected monkeys, they'd have died out years ago!" he snapped back – but there was a flicker in his eyes. He was suddenly a lot more sober.

"That's right," added Bokhani. "We're the aliens here – we're the ones with no immunity..." He'd obviously been thinking about it.

"I hope you're right!" Yukashi went back to looking down into the lake. Keeping both hands firmly in contact with the rail, she leaned out as far as she dared, shuffling aft, fingers sliding along the polished metal. She reached the stern without spotting anything – not even floating wood – and began to relax slightly. But as she rounded the stern and started moving forward again, she saw something dark and smooth nudged up against the boat's side.

She stared at it for half a minute, willing the shape to be

something else – but she couldn't deny it. It was a body. A human body. And human corpses floating on the surface aren't the victims of crocs or hippos.

She remembered the three men De Broek shot two nights ago.

"Get a boat-hook or something!" she yelled. "Anything we can reach it with!"

Both men were by her side moments later.

"You want to bring it on board?" said De Broek.

"Are you mad?" Yukashi was incredulous. "I want it as far from us as possible!"

Bokhani rushed off to find a boat-hook. Then Edmund Adjatay himself appeared from below.

"What's happening?" he called.

"There's a floating corpse pressing up against the boat," Yukashi replied. "The current must be holding it there."

"Does Lake Tego have a current?" De Broek wondered softly.

Adjatay joined them at the side. He glanced down once, then backed off, his olive skin turning an unpleasant grey.

"Get rid of it!" he hissed.

"That's the plan," De Broek said with bleak humour.

Bokhani returned with a boat-hook, but after only a couple of attempts it was obviously not long enough.

"You'll have to try from a lower deck window," said De Broek, grinning at the African with a skeletal leer.

"Go to hell!" muttered Bokhani. "This is as close as I go—"

"Get rid of it!" there was a brittle edge to Adjatay's voice. "Get rid of it!"

De Broek disappeared below. Yukashi looked at Adjatay's tense, stretched face. He looked like he was screaming mutely.

"Move the boat, Mr Adjatay," she said, trying to sound as reasonable as possible. "Back it off – whatever. Just move us away."

"We're not moving anywhere!" He glared at her, his features so rigid she thought they might snap if he tried to move them.

"We have to do something!"

"We're not moving!"

De Broek was suddenly between them, shouldering them aside without ceremony. He raised his Mauser rifle and carefully, meticulously, fired at the corpse. It jerked, twitched as though still alive, rolled in the water. As De Broek emptied a clip into it, it began to founder. Then, with a final roll, it sank into the muddy water.

De Broek slung the rifle over a shoulder. "Just needed puncturing," he said, almost cheerfully. As he walked away he glanced back over his shoulder. "Oi – *kaffir* – get that bloody jungle music back on again! This party's dying…"

\*

There was one other boat on board the *Busiris*. Hardly a lifeboat – Adjatay would never sail his yacht anywhere likely to need one. It was more like a small cabin cruiser, perched on the *Busiris*'s superstructure like a whale calf against its mother. Yukashi doubted Adjatay had even used it.

De Broek and Bokhani were growing louder as their liquor consumption grew. The CD player could be felt through the deck. Adjatay had gone below again – back to his black cinema. Yukashi felt that the jungle's silence had nothing to do with the throbbing rap – it had grown watchful, expectant. The body against the boat had been some kind of offering – and she didn't know if they'd accepted it properly.

She climbed the short ladder up the deck holding the smaller launch. It was simply held in place by locked davits. Released, they swung the launch over the *Busiris*'s starboard side and lowered it into the water. Simple, and entirely automatic.

Yukashi found the small white box that contained the switch. Flipping up a cover, she thumbed the green button underneath. Motors hummed in a no-nonsense manner, and the davits rotated the launch out across the superstructure. It swung gently in its supports; Yukashi had to stop herself

85

giggling when it occurred to her it was swaying in time to the music below.

She ducked back down the ladder and half-ran towards De Broek and Bokhani. They were singing something that had little to do with the rap, conducting themselves with dribbling bottles of scotch – but their words were completely drowned. Yukashi tugged at Bokhani's shirtsleeve. He turned and looked at her, blearily.

"Let's go!" she yelled over the pounding music. "I've got the launch out... We can go..."

"Where to?" Bokhani shouted back. His eyes were alight and dancing – but it didn't look like amusement. Not this time. "It's everywhere, lady! You think you're immune, or something?" He turned his back on her, taking a pull at his scotch.

Yukashi stifled another giggle. Why not? She'd been exposed the longest of any on board the *Busiris* – she'd touched Burrell Makelele. But she wasn't symptomatic – not yet. And everyone else had exhibited symptoms and died within hours – not days. But she couldn't bring herself to say it.

"We can get help – bring it back for Mr Adjatay...!"

De Broek laughed – a harsh sound that had no humour in it. "Forget it, lady," he shouted. "We're having a good time." He wiped his sweating, flushed face. "You want to go – go. And take fucking Adjatay with you!" He took a swig of his own bottle, realised it was empty, and tossed it overboard. "He can take your mind off the trip..." He made crude thrusting gestures with a fist, then staggered away – looking for more drink, Yukashi assumed.

She left them to it, not sure what else to say – even if she'd had the nerve to say it. She went below, making her way down to where Adjatay was in the darkness, watching his own stuff of dreams dancing across the screen. The rap from on deck was so loud, it even penetrated the black theatre, adding a primal throb to the movie's own score.

"Mr Adjatay," she called to no response. "I'm leaving. I'm taking the launch and going. Now. I'll send help as soon as I get to the western shore."

Adjatay remained silent.

Yukashi stalked through the dark room, shaking but determined. He didn't glance at her when she stood before him – his eyes never once left the screen.

"Goodbye, Mr Adjatay," Yukashi said – but he was on another island completely. She balled her fists – grinding her nails into her palms – and started to leave.

"'And my ending is despair,'" she heard him say – a thin, emaciated voice she didn't recognise. She glanced at him again – and saw the blood running from his eyes and ears, the black sweat beginning to well up from his paling face.

She ran through the door, pulling desperately on it as it closed in its own, deadly slow time. As she rushed up to the deck, the music beat out a slow counter-measure to her freewheeling heart. The air was sweet and heavy with rot and decay; the shadows aped trunks and vines. They hadn't escaped the jungle – it had come for them.

De Broek and Bokhani were oblivious – lost in their own doomed invocations against death. Yukashi made for the launch, dragging herself clumsily over the *Busiris*'s rail, dropping the several feet onto the launch's deck with no grace. She started up the engines, cast off from the davits, and opened the throttle as wide as it would go.

She'd bring back no help – there was none to be had. Only fire – napalm, that would do it. Burn the plague out just like they'd burned back the jungle.

She swung the wheel, leaving the *Busiris* far behind. Eventually the beat of the rap became the launch's engines, and the slap of the lake. Behind her, the jungle breathed and sighed. She smelled its rank heat; felt a tickle as something warm ran from her nose

# ON THE COUCH

## Craig Herbertson

Mulliner raised himself from the psychologist's couch. The psychologist had gone. The room was empty. Through the half open door, Mulliner could see a brightly lit corridor lined with rows of shut doors; like sentinels standing guard. From where he sat the doors seemed small. This, and the fact that they were all shut, were the two thoughts that struck him; both depressive thoughts; the kind of thoughts he was here to have removed, or at least cast back into the recesses of his mind.

And where was the psychologist, Dr Brixton? The man being paid a lot of money to cure him. Mulliner rubbed the back of his neck and sat upright. He could feel tension, here in his neck and, more deeply placed, a muted ache in his forehead. The agony was dulled now but he remembered it at its electric strength. The strength it bore when it had prostrated him some weeks before.

Mulliner returned his gaze to the immediate surroundings. Dr Brixton's desk, the small table with the bowl of fruit on it, the Cezanne echoing the fruit, and the comfortable chair where the good doctor usually propped himself. None of it had changed. There was even a sheaf of manila on the large desk. It had been there when Dr Brixton had begun the session. Mulliner remembered it.

For that, he felt grateful. Of late, his memory had been poor. It was not that his faculties were fading. It was more that they were becoming uncertain.

It had begun with the dreams. Mulliner winced. He felt his body cringe with an irrepressible fear. When it passed, after a few moments, he found he had bitten his lip. The blood tasted dry and salt in his mouth and he could already feel a swelling, internal cut. He felt ashamed; ashamed of the fear.

But the dreams unnerved him and he hated to be alone.

Where the hell was Dr Brixton?

88

*On the Couch*

He rose cautiously to his feet; flinching at the vertigo that overtook him. Then he walked to the far window. Dr Brixton always kept the windows shuttered. The bright light bothered Mulliner and now on impulse he wanted to see the view from the window. It had been sunny outside when he had first entered the asylum. From this side of the building he ought to be able to see over the common pasture; perhaps even as far as the line of elms marking Brooks River.

But the shutter was stuck. He examined the connecting cord. There seemed to be a knot in it obstructing the passage of the cord and preventing the shutter's movement. It was a simple enough explanation; Dr Brixton had been unable to open the shutter because of the fault. It was not some quixotic preference for claustrophobic rooms. However, the mood that Mulliner found himself in defied the logic of the explanation. He had a sudden apprehension that there was nothing behind the shutter. If he attempted to wrench it open he would find a brick wall or perhaps something worse; nothingness or a cadaver decomposing into green slime.

He backed away from the window. Sweat ran down his brow. Then, recovering himself, he sat back on the couch. The worn leather felt strange and clammy against his palms, like a living thing. It was an unpleasant sensation but he needed to rest. Again he could see down the angle of the corridor. He could watch the retreating perspective of the doors; doors that grew progressively smaller until they were lost to sight; doors beyond which, he assumed, there were other rooms much like this one. Other Dr Brixtons, other Mulliners; treaters and those being treated.

The comforting assumption that he was part of a community of ill people being cured quickly dissipated. There was no reason to assume that any of the doors contained anything. Like this room they might be devoid of psychiatrists, might even be devoid of life.

The agony of mind came rolling in like a black sea.

It occurred to Mulliner that to relieve the pain he must open the window and see the view. If he broke the shutter he broke it. He had money; he could pay for a new one. If Dr Brixton thought he was being aggressive he could explain that it had broken when he tried to open it.

He heard a noise, far away. A distant whistle, soft and tuneless. The tiny doors seemed to shimmer as though the view through the half open door of his room was a view through deep yet translucent water; as though the deep water had been disturbed. He shook his head, trying to shake out the nausea and convince himself that he was a solid object. For a moment, he had felt insubstantial. Or rather, that the world that he inhabited was insubstantial and that he was a transparent creature of a transparent world.

Mulliner rose again from the couch and attacked the shutter.

At first the Formica panels resisted him. He tore at the cords and then punched out, breaking through. With a shout of exertion, he pushed his hands in the gap and wrenched.

It was worse than he had expected.

Behind the shutter there was a painting of a psychologist's room. The tableau was familiar. It was the precise tableau enacted in Dr Brixton's room.

And the central character was Mulliner; the despairing Mulliner.

He heard the low whistle far away.

And then he woke to find a menacing figure looming over him.

But it was only Dr Brixton.

The psychologist smiled at him with a look of professional concern. "Relax. It is over now. Remain calm and try to relax."

"This time it was a room. It's never been a room before. It was awful."

Dr Brixton thrust an optometer into Mulliner's eye and began annotating in his wrist computer.

"It's certainly a new development, the use of a more concrete symbolism, but I'm sure it's nothing we can't deal with." He flicked the light off and rubbed his small chin. "Shall we return to the list of characters who currently inhabit your dreams?"

"There's the girl…"

"Name them. It will help."

"Siren, then. Siren is the one that eats my private parts and spews them out over my chest."

"Yes, a particularly unpleasant dream for you, but the eating and regurgitation is simply a symbolic representation of rebirth. Your manhood, specifically in this case your ego, is under threat. Once you have come to terms with the threat and have accommodated it into your psyche your personality will be reborn, hence the regurgitation."

Mulliner gulped, unconvinced. "Then there's the Twins. One chases me over the bridge and just when I'm across his brother appears at the other side… carrying a torch—"

"And burns you up," Dr Brixton interrupted. "Again, the bridge is a subconscious picture of a crisis which you must face and then cross, the Twins—"

"Damn it, Dr Brixton! The Twins are real. I know they are. You haven't been in these dreams. You've only heard my version."

Dr Brixton smiled indulgently. "The dreams are real to you Mulliner, of course they are. Even if I think they are manifestations of an internal reality set up by your unconscious, we can still talk rationally about them. And never forget, you came here to get rid of these unpleasant dreams. That is what we are going to do. It doesn't matter how we define the battleground."

Mulliner did not like the smile. If Dr Brixton had managed to say these things without the smile he would have felt a lot happier.

In the afternoon the patients went out into the fresh air whether they liked it or not. Mulliner hated exercise and normally chose to spend the afternoon playing draughts with Miss Ferris on the paved board. The board was in the veranda just beneath Dr Brixton's room and today Mulliner couldn't rid himself of the feeling that the room was peering over his shoulder. He decided on a whim to walk as far as Brooks River. Miss Ferris walked with him.

Mulliner didn't like Miss Ferris. She was plain and chinless and her hair was too long for a woman of her age. However, as far as he was concerned she had two saving graces. She was good at draughts and she was obsessed with dreams and their significance. The obsession had resulted in her recommendation to the institution but it also meant that she would listen for hours to Mulliner's dream descriptions.

He unburdened the latest nightmare. Miss Ferris nodded thoughtfully now and again, and when he had finished, they walked in silence for some time before she spoke.

"I'm interested in this whistle. What kind of whistle was it?"

"Eh?"

"Was it a 'hello' whistle? An appreciative whistle?"

"Oh. Let me think. It was a call I think. Yes, almost like a dog owner calling a dog." Mulliner grimaced. The idea of being summoned like a dog did not appeal to him.

"Did you respond to the call, follow it?"

"No. I just wanted to get out. I felt that the pains in my head would be relieved if I did. I opened the shutter. Then I saw...?"

"What you saw was your doppelganger."

"My doppelganger?"

"Yes, your shadow self, but you didn't get a close look. You woke too soon. You should have faced it."

"It's easy for you to say. You weren't there."

"Also, you broke through the shutter. You didn't take the proper steps. Your doppelganger called you. You could have met on even terms by following the whistle. You should have met it in the corridor."

"But I saw that... thing in the window tableaux. It was like me but it wasn't me. It was horrific, threatening."

"Yes, but you abstracted it from you by placing it outside the window. Dream incidents are all contrived by yourself, you know? God sets the ground rules for your spiritual journey. But you supply the permutations. I had a similar experience several years ago…"

But Mulliner didn't want to hear. As they walked, he thought about Dr Brixton's room. He didn't really like his doctor, but the feeling of dislike always intensified in the room where he worked.

They reached Brooks River, and Miss Ferris was still talking about God.

From far away the river had always attracted Mulliner. It was pleasant to see the trees that lined the horizon and to think that they marked a boundary. Like his mind. If only he could cross the boundary he would be in the fantasy land beyond, happy. But close up, the river was a disappointment. It was a drainage sewer. A grill, choked with plastic bags and paper cups, blocked its passage. The trees had been barked by someone and would die in the winter.

Mulliner picked up a stick, using it to try and remove one of the plastic bags to allow freer passage for the water. It was useless. He threw the stick away. "It's Dr Brixton's room I don't like. I think that's the source of the trouble. You know, the more I think about it the more I think my dreams weren't all that bad before I came to this damn place. You know what I'm going to do. I'm going to search Dr Brixton's room. I bet there's a dead rat in there or something, or no air conditioning. I'm going to cure myself. You coming?"

Diligently Miss Ferris followed.

The institution was quiet. The good weather had attracted the nurses out on to the lawns. Feeling like a naughty schoolchild, Mulliner entered the building with Miss Ferris following.

There was a bad atmosphere in Dr Brixton's room. Miss Ferris scented it immediately. They checked everywhere by hand, looking through files, under the table, behind the shutter.

They found nothing. Then Miss Ferris tried dowsing for evil, a technique she had adapted from the seventies journal, *Man, Myth and Magic*. She found a source emanating from around the couch. Mulliner tapped the floors and walls, and finally found the trouble.

There was a false section to the wall.

It was at this juncture that a noise interrupted them; nurses coming back from their break. They made a run for it and arranged to try again after the evening session.

The low whistle echoed down the corridor. The shutter was still down, and although Mulliner knew he was dreaming, the knowledge didn't stop him from being thoroughly scared. He examined the tableaux.

The scene was fixed. The first time he had seen it he thought the doppelganger was about to move. Now, from a distance he could see that it was simply a very clever scenario. Poised on its feet, the creature looked set to jump. When he walked closer he saw that it bore little resemblance to himself. It was wearing a rubber mask.

The dream was vivid but he could still remember Miss Ferris's advice. He had to go down the corridor; confront his doppelganger. Then everything would be fine. The bad dreams would stop and he would be able to return to work. He was about to turn and walk down the corridor when the doppelganger spoke. It said, "Wake up Mulliner."

The doppelganger was Dr Brixton.

Mulliner was annoyed. "I felt for once I was getting somewhere. I was in control and then you have to wake me up."

"You seem to forget it was only a dream. You are treating it like a waking sensation." Dr Brixton walked toward the shuttered window twirling his optometer. "It may be that drugs are the only solution. I didn't want to recommend them initially, but…"

"I felt that if I only saw this figure in the corridor, if I faced it, I would be cured – all those nightmares, all those evil people in my dreams. They're not products of my imagination. Goddamn it they're real."

"To you," said Dr Brixton. He wrote something in his file.

Miss Ferris bounced her draught over two of Mulliner's. "I think Dr Brixton is wrong. Drugs are a mistake. If only you had confronted—"

"But I didn't, and the nightmares go on. The Siren, the Twins…"

"Your own body defences are your best protection. Tonight we can break into Dr Brixton's room. We'll open that hollow place and I'll perform an exorcism."

"Tonight," said Mulliner emphatically.

Mulliner brought the trowel, the flashlight, the stolen hammer and plaster-mix to repair the hole. Miss Ferris brought the chalk, the candles, the salt and the sanctified water. Breaking in was easy enough. In fact, it was easier than stealing the equipment that had already delayed the operation by some hours. Mulliner had a natural talent for picking locks already demonstrated on the caretaker's store cupboard. The whole episode would have been fun for Mulliner if it hadn't been for Miss Ferris's grim visage and the memory of the dreams. For several hours, they worked on the hole. At first, they had suspected that it would lead to a hollow cupboard but it soon became apparent that an entire room lay concealed behind the plaster. The news excited Miss Ferris. "It could be a dark sanctuary for a witches' Sabbat. You'd better let me go first."

Mulliner consented.

After a few minutes, in which he sweated alone in Dr Brixton's room, Mulliner heard Miss Ferris call for him to come through. He sent up a silent prayer and crawled through the small gap.

Inside was a room smaller than Dr Brixton's. It was deserted and had been for some time. Mulliner recognised the trappings of a previous era of psychiatry. Dust overlay leather-bound volumes, silver objects and implements. There was a pump and hose, which he guessed, might be for force-feeding. The whole place reeked of the past. Mulliner wanted to get out as quickly as he could but Miss Ferris had found something.

"There's a drawer full of old files here. This may be the answer to your problems."

"Can we just get away from here?"

"No, here's the name of the psychiatrist. Billings. Winter Billings. What a name."

Mulliner felt the old nausea forcing its way up from his stomach.

"Sounds awful to me. Can we leave?"

"I'm going to take some of these files. There's not many. I can actually sense the spirit world seeping out from the pages. I've never had such a vivid experience of… evil."

"Can't you just leave them and get us out of here?"

"No, Mr Mulliner." She turned to face him, her long hair obscuring her chin and making her look unexpectedly attractive. "These files could provide the solution to your problem."

Mulliner spent an hour cosmetically plastering the hole. He had hoped the presentiment of evil would disappear with the hole but it remained lodged in his mind until he left Dr Brixton's room. Miss Ferris had gone to inspect the files. Mulliner was quite happy to leave her to delve into the evil and report back the next morning.

He got up late and had a breakfast of cereal, hot buttered toast and strong, hot coffee. From his window, the trees at Brooks river looked pleasantly shady. He considered going for a long walk with Miss Ferris. She wasn't such a bad stick; she had even looked vaguely attractive the night before. They could discuss his dreams. Mulliner felt some confidence now in her 'Sensitivity', an ability he had thought to be palpable nonsense until she had discovered the room. He decided to call on her.

Two orderlies stopped him at the door to her room.

"What's up?" Mulliner asked.

He had to wait for Dr Brixton to emerge before he got an answer.

"I shouldn't say, professional discretion... but you are her friend... Miss Ferris took a bad turn last night. What she calls her 'Sensitivity', her morbid interest in the occult. It seems she was overcome and fainted."

"Is she okay?"

"Oh, she's fine. Just needs some rest and then we can probably pick up where we left off. I'm afraid it will be a long haul with her though..."

"She didn't say what had... upset her did she?"

"That's the curious thing. She was raving about Winter Billings, a rather notorious quack who practised here about ninety years ago. I've no idea where she got her information."

"Billings. What was wrong with Billings?" Mulliner felt a nasty lump in his throat.

"Nothing much. He didn't cure his patients. He ensured that they went completely round the twist. No one knows how he managed to do it. They know why; money of course, got them all to fund his practise and became very rich."

"He doesn't sound like much of an advert for psychiatry. What happened to him?"

"You'll be pleased to hear that he got his comeuppance. They found him lying on his own couch, a gibbering wreck. Never recovered."

Dr Brixton smiled. "Don't look so worried Mr Mulliner, all that nonsense went out with the Victorians."

"Did it?"

"Time for your session I think?"

Mulliner heard the whistle before he opened his eyes. It was snaking down the corridor. The fear was still there; it had come on him as soon as Dr Brixton had opened the door and pointed to the couch. Now, in the dream it was intensifying. He staggered to his feet and lurched to the water basin, splashing the water on his face to try and wake up. But it was useless. Dr Brixton had drugged him before sending him under. He shouldn't feel this sense of reality.

Not a dream.

A nightmare.

Crawling from beneath the couch was Siren. If she got to him, she would be hungry. Her red lips would descend to trouser level and... He backed away trying to reach the door. The first of the Twins burst through the shutter. The second twin he could see carrying the torch.

The only way out was the corridor. And blocking the doorway was The Cat, a corpse-like harlot with shadow eyes and a gleaming hat pin. Mulliner took a dive at her feet. She toppled over him stabbing at his exposed back but fear lent him strength and he was through to the corridor and running like a trained athlete.

He could smell the dreadful smell of cheap perfume cloying on his clothes. The scent was ancient and grotesque, as though someone had skimped on the quality of incense at a funeral. The breath burnt in his lungs as he raced towards the exit of the institution.

There was someone ahead. A figure he did not recognise. A spare man clad in old-fashioned weeds like an undertaker. His dreams had never given this figure an airing before. Unlike Mulliner, he looked thin and weak. Mulliner knew this was the one dream figure between nightmare and awakening; although it bore little resemblance to him, it must be his doppelganger. He felt capable of handling it.

Until he saw the eyes.

Mulliner slowed, turned around. The Cat was crawling. The Twins were jostling to climb her and he could just discern the Siren licking blood red lips. There was no escape except past this new figure.

"Mr Mulliner." The voice had emerged from its mouth like a snail from a shell. Unwillingly, Mulliner faced the figure.

"You're safe with me, Mr Mulliner. I've been waiting for you… to cure you. These dreadful nightmares you've been having." The figure was slinking towards him on mantis legs. Mulliner couldn't avert his face from the compelling gaze. "If you just come this way. I assure you you're in safe hands…" The thing pulled a device from its pocket, some sort of silver talisman hung on a string. Its spindle hands spun the talisman and a peculiar whistling suffused the corridor. Mulliner felt his eyes drawn to the device, his mind melting under the gaze of the man he had just recognised.

He whispered, "It can't be."

But it was.


Dr Brixton looked in on Miss Ferris later that evening. It had been a tiring day and he wished it were over. Mrs Brixton always cooked fish on Fridays and fish was his favourite. Good food was just the thing; helped the constitution and fish was especially good for the brain. He needed to think hard about the practice after dinner. It had been a very bad day.

Miss Ferris was sitting up on the small bed, her thin hands clenching and unclenching. When Dr Brixton entered, she threw back her long hair and tried to compose herself. "I've worked it out," she said. "We were wrong about the room"

"Please, Miss Ferris, I don't think we should be discussing it. You're on edge—"

"There is nothing wrong with me. I have simply discovered something terrible and wish to inform the appropriate authorities."

"What have you discovered Miss Ferris? A few old files."

"They're Billings's files and you know it."

"They may be, and if so, they are merely historical documents."

"They're much more than that." Miss Ferris rose to her feet and paced the room. "They show step by step how Billings lured his victims to madness. How he practised some occult science on them through hypnosis; perhaps some sort of dream invasion induced by drugs by which he inserted his own persona into the victim's subconscious—"

"Really Miss Ferris. You came here to dispel these illusions."

"They're not illusions, damn you." Miss Ferris's weak chin trembled. "You haven't looked through the files, examined them in detail. I have."

Dr Brixton shook his head.

"Mr Mulliner and I thought it was the hidden room," continued Miss Ferris. "That was our big mistake. I felt the evil emanate from that area and then Mr Mulliner found the hollow. That's what threw me. It wasn't the room."

"Please take a seat. This is only upsetting you."

"No I won't take a seat. The only thing that's upsetting me is your stupidity. Can't you see? It wasn't the room at all. It was the couch."

"The couch?" Dr Brixton blinked.

"Yes, the old leather couch. It's Billings's couch, the original. The couch where they found Billings crazed out of his mind."

"I suppose it could be; some of the fittings are original. But what does it matter if it is original?"

"Because the couch has something inside it, a device, a talisman, a thing of power." Miss Ferris sat down exhausted.

Dr Brixton stared into space searching for his confident manner, thinking abstractly of fish garnished with parsley.

"I have a theory that Winter Billings set up the power himself as a kind of web to ensnare the minds of his victims. But the mad personae themselves were embedded in the couch. Each persona haunted the next victim until he or she succumbed. Eventually, the weaker personae would be drained or devoured by the stronger minds. That's what got Billings in the end. Perhaps he sat on the couch one night by mistake or maybe something lured him there. In any event, he was dragged in and succumbed. My God, Doctor! Winter Billings must still be in there…" Miss Ferris turned to Dr Brixton. "You must believe me. You have got to stop treating poor Mr Mulliner on that couch."

"If it makes you feel better I will find an appropriate alternative."

"I'm relieved Dr Brixton, thank you. You will examine those files. Won't you?"

"Later."

Dr Brixton walked out on to the driveway. It had been a dreadful day. He had felt it best not to tell Miss Ferris about Mulliner's true condition. If she knew of his hopeless collapse during the last session, it might really tip her over the edge.

God knows how she would react knowing Mulliner had been left strapped to the couch.

# THE CRIMSON PICTURE

## Daniel McGachey

On those infrequent occasions that my good friend, Dr Lawrence, can be prised away from his antiquarian researches for an hour or two of leisure, his tastes incline rather more to the jollity of the music hall or thrills of the picture palace than such loftier diversions as the opera, museum or art gallery. Museums are, after all, where he spends much of his time as a matter of daily course. While the art gallery holds little pleasure since, after so many years of peering at figures woven into illuminated manuscripts, frozen in stained glass or poised as gargoyles on church roof or crypt, he occasionally feels them peering back at him. As for the opera; of that he will only offer the cryptic response that the shrieking is altogether too reminiscent of things he would prefer not to be put once more in mind of.

It was something of a surprise, therefore, when the porter knocked upon his study door and presented Lawrence with a card inviting him to a private viewing at an art gallery located at an exclusive address in the city. Why such an invitation should come to him he could not fathom. Was there, perhaps, some mix up? Maybe there was a similarly named fellow in the arts faculty? The porter assured him that there was not and, feeling ill-suited to assist in the solving of the puzzle, took his leave; grumbling all the way of how he knew exactly who was who in the college and why shouldn't he know him, after all those heavy old books and musty packages, some from suspiciously foreign sounding places, he'd delivered over the years?

Lawrence turned the perplexing matter over in his mind and, while doing so, also happened to turn the card over in his hands and there, in rather fussily elaborate handwriting, he had his answer. It read:

*My dear Lawrence,*

## The Crimson Picture

*If you remember your old classmate Drayton with any affection, kindly join me at the address on the front of this invitation at your earliest convenience. The matter is a peculiar one and such was always your forte.*

*Sincerely yours,*
*H. D.*

"Horace Drayton," Lawrence recalled, casting his mind back a good number of years to a classroom filled with eager... though some not so eager... young faces. His mind's eye affixed itself to one particular face, capped with a tangle of unruly black curls and smudged on the side of the nose with a stripe of green paint that no amount of rubbing with a spittle-flecked finger would shift. "Ah, yes, he always was the artistic one." When a second glance at the front of the card showed his name, not as the subject of the current exhibition but as the proprietor of the gallery, it tended to confirm the rest of his memory, that Drayton's enthusiasm for art had outstripped his ability. But he had always been a determined lad and, in spite of his sadly deficient facility, that determination to surround himself with the type of work that brought him such pleasure had clearly been strong.

There was, then, some admiration in Lawrence's smile of greeting and approval in the firmness of his handshake when, after both train journey and tram ride, he presented himself at the address on the card and was shown directly to the proprietor's office, there to be met by Horace Drayton.

Although several decades had now passed since last they had set eyes upon one another, there was no mistaking Lawrence's former associate. The hair may have been greyer and more styled and anointed but it still looked set to spring at any moment into wild curls. Indeed, so little had changed that Lawrence could not help but look for a tell-tale smudge and, in next to no time, his gaze had Mr Drayton nervously rubbing at the side of his nose, asking, "Is there something on my face?"

"Not at all," beamed Lawrence, the friend of childhood memory now complete and in the flesh before him. "I'm merely amazed that so little has changed for you after such a long time. Well, yes, the clothes are finer and better cut than the old uniform and this office is a sight more comfortable than the upper corridor dorm, but you seem hardly to have aged. Some of us have felt the full force of the years," and here his hand strayed to his own prematurely whitened hair. "Yet look at you! Tell me, you don't happen to have an enchanted portrait of yourself tucked away in an attic like the fellow in that Wilde story?"

At this, the signs of strain showed themselves with such rapidity on that smooth and youthful face that, for one moment, Lawrence thought that Drayton was indeed going to admit that, yes, he did possess such an object. And his next words did little to dispel that notion.

"There is a picture I would like you to look at. Whether or not it is enchanted I cannot say, though that seems altogether too benevolent a word. But, such things were always your area of interest. Perhaps you might tell me if there is indeed something unnatural in it. I'll confess it, the thing fills me with the deepest dread even to look at it… or have it look back at me." With which sentiments Lawrence, thinking again of those saintly faces in glass or hellish minions in stone, could only sympathise.

"Perhaps, though," Drayton conceded, "there really is nothing there and it is only fancy on my part after hearing the incredible story that goes with this work. But then, when you have heard the tale, you too might also see a fathomless horror in every swirl and whorl of paint."

"Then there is a story behind this intriguing summons?" queried Lawrence, his interest, as ever, piqued by the mere suggestion of some fresh piece of lore to add to his already compendious store of uncanny chronicles.

"There is certainly a story," sighed the gallery proprietor. "But I shall not be the one to tell it. I think it better that you

104

hear it, in all its detail, from the one who told me. You might find it unbelievable. I know I did. At least, I wished I did. But he swears it is true, that the events he describes happened to him and, when you hear it and see that picture... I mean really look into the heart of it..." His voice tailed off and a sickly look etched itself across his features.

"Very well," said Lawrence, "and when am I to meet the narrator of this remarkable tale?"

"Shortly. He lives not too far distant and I told my assistant to fetch him the instant you arrived." Rising from behind his desk, and bidding Lawrence to follow, he ventured, "Perhaps it will be of use, while we await him, for me to tell you of the circumstances whereby he shared his testimony with me."

"Indeed so," Lawrence agreed and he followed his old schoolmate from the office and back into the plush gallery area.

"As you can see, we are host to quite an exclusive exhibition at the moment," declared Drayton, a trace of pride beginning to replace the frown of worry on his face, as he threw his arms wide, indicating the walls bedecked with canvasses in their ornate, gilded frames. Lawrence glanced politely at the gaudy landscapes and stern portraits, though his attention was reserved for the unfolding account. "Some of the most prestigious names working today are grouped under this roof. It has been a long and complicated process in arranging such a gathering. But not every piece is here simply because of the fame of its originator. As you may gather, my own hoped-for-talent never flourished, alas. But there are those whose faculty did take hold, only to find it hidden by undeserved obscurity. By mingling the celebrated masters with these deserving cases, it was my hope that their lights may be allowed to shine a little brighter."

Drayton selected a lavish catalogue from a side table and opened it to a certain page, before handing it to his guest with a sigh of, "There is one picture I wish I had never brought before human eyes."

## The Crimson Picture

The title in the catalogue was given as: '*Unknown Subject –
A Portrait In Crimson – Oil On Canvas – Artist Anonymous.*'

"But this cannot be right, surely?" Lawrence said,
perplexed. "If you hope to showcase some neglected talents
then withholding the name of one whom you would wish to
celebrate seems hardly helpful."

"Ah, yes," Drayton accepted, "but that was to be my
surprise. You see, officially the artist's identity is unknown;
the work is unsigned. But I know him. I have an old friend who
made a name for himself for a short time some years back. I've
displayed as much work of his as I could find room for in the
past but, of late, he has not enjoyed any great success and has
sold off most of what he once produced at a pittance merely to
keep body and soul together. So, as soon as I first set eyes on
the portrait, I recognised my friend's handiwork, even if the
style is somewhat more... fantastical than his more
acknowledged work.

"How splendid, thought I, to have found one of his forgotten
commissions. Would it not be a grand surprise for him,
receiving an invitation to mingle with artistically minded
persons at the opening of an exhibition, to then discover that
his own creation was to be the centrepiece that would direct
the limelight once more upon him?"

Here the proprietor paused and, turning to a young man who
was taking great pains in the delicate adjustment of those
scarlet ropes in their brass holders that would keep the
evening's patrons at a safe remove from the paintings, said,
"Ernest, could you run along and fetch that newspaper?"

The lad scurried off toward the reception desk and Lawrence
prompted, "And were you correct? Was your friend
surprised?"

Drayton laughed, a humourless bark, and when the youth
returned with a folded over newspaper, he merely tilted his
head to indicate that Lawrence was to receive the journal.
When it was handed to him, the first thing that caught his eye
was the headline: '*Commotion at Exhibition Opening.*'

"Ah," Lawrence nodded, "I skimmed this just this morning, though, of course, it was before your summons arrived and I had no idea it was connected with you at the time. Someone going berserk and attempting to slash one of the paintings, if I remember right? Then I must surmise the intended target to be your mysterious crimson picture."

"You do remember right and surmise correctly. This is the very painting here," Drayton said. They had come to a halt before what was clearly a large canvas, though its subject was obscured by the red silk which hung over it. "And the man who attacked it, or, at least, attempted to attack it, was the artist, Hector Jardine."

On seeing Lawrence's blank look, the gallery owner supplied the information that Mr Hector Jardine had enjoyed a measure of celebrity for a series of landscapes, "Where," Drayton explained, "the figures were as much a feature as the landscapes themselves, humanity and nature, joyful, fruitful and alive."

But, before he could present a comprehensive discourse on the artist's life and works, a lilting voice cut in, declaring, "I am hardly surprised that your guest has not heard of me, Horace. My fame, such as it was, was minor and fleeting."

"Hector," exclaimed Drayton, rushing forward to greet the speaker. "I'm so very glad you could come."

"I'm surprised you would want me back here after my... after the incident." The new arrival on the scene was stooped, though not from age as Lawrence judged him to be several years younger than Drayton and he. Yet the face, seen at closer quarters when the man came forward, was careworn and the eyes weary. His clothing, though evidently expensive, was showing signs of fraying and, from the style and cut, it was apparent that his fleeting moment of prosperity had been some twenty or more years previous. The general impression was that here was a man worn down and beaten by some terrible burden. He looked utterly incapable of the violent outburst with which he was credited. Yet, by all accounts he had smashed a champagne bottle and made to slash to ribbons the painting beneath the silk.

"This is the fellow I told you about, Hector," said Drayton, presenting a somewhat guarded Lawrence to the placid looking man who was nevertheless apparently capable of random eruptions of fury. "He may be able to help, if you were but to give him your account."

"You haven't told him?" Jardine's words were a reluctant sigh.

"I thought not to," Drayton explained. "At best, I could sketch in the basics but, were you to tell him what you told me last night, you would paint a much more vivid picture."

The artist allowed himself a wry smile at Drayton's carefully selected phrasing. But it was gone from his lips as the proprietor made a move to lift the covering silk from the painting. "Please, leave it covered, I beg of you. If I am to gaze upon it as I tell the tale, I fear I may have the urge to finish what I was prevented from doing last night!"

Nodding, Drayton allowed the silk to drop back, so that all Lawrence glimpsed of the canvas was the fleeting impression of a hand, clutching and veined, bathed in a glow of blood red intensity, the fingers contorted almost into claws. Despite being still in his overcoat and scarf, he found himself shivering as he pondered that if this mere corner of the piece was so powerful in its grotesquery, what dreadfulness must the rest of the painting possess?

By the time Lawrence's eyes were drawn once more from the square of silk before him, he found that the artist had placed himself on a chair facing directly toward the covered canvas. Thus seated, he began, without further bidding, to share his most singular confession.

*

My story begins conventionally enough, I should imagine, when, as a young man, I had defied the wishes of my parents by embarking on a career... no, a calling, as an artist. They had entertained every expectation that I would enter one of the professions; either legal, as my father's kin tended to be, or medical in the footsteps of my maternal grandfather. But the law held no interest for me and I was more inclined toward capturing an impression of the life essence than studying the science of it.

Thus we find me eating when I can afford it, attempting to sleep through the hunger when I cannot; the rest of the time spent painting, practising, honing whatever gift I may have possessed. Oftentimes it was a choice between food and fresh supplies of paint. It was an easy choice. "I will eat tomorrow," I reasoned, "but I cannot guarantee that I will be inspired tomorrow so, today, I paint!"

Sometimes my mother would send me money, insisting that I accept it that she might rest assured that no son of hers was going to become destitute. You see, my parents may have been distant and reserved, proud, even, but they were far from the heartless monsters that one reads of in melodrama and tragedy. There was no disinheritance, no banishment or estrangement. While they may not have entirely understood my passion, the money was there should I have need of it. But it was I who refused to take it! My pride, you see; my determination that I would succeed on talent alone.

But pride doesn't put a roof over a man's head or food in his belly, does it? Consequently, when I was neither painting nor sleeping, I took what employment came to hand. Not jobs requiring hard, intense labour. As anyone looking at me could tell, I've hardly the build or stamina for it. Besides which, would I dare take on a task that might damage my hands and prevent my painting? No, the work was mainly in restaurants and public houses. In one or two, the landlords would even allow me to display some of my work and I actually earned small commissions from the customers. Some were looking for a likeness, usually of a sweetheart or child. Others might offer a few pennies for a sketch in pencil or chalk. I accepted all

109

requests, no matter the fee. After all, while money was welcome, the chance to practice my skills was a matter of necessity.

But the man who was waiting for me on that October night, as the last of the regulars left and I prepared to lock up the bar, was not a customer I had ever set eyes on before.

I was not even aware of his presence until he spoke. "You are the artist, I presume?" Yet his curiously assured voice suggested that he already knew the answer. He was tall and lean, clad neatly in black from head to toe, in clothes that seemed to attract neither dust specks nor wrinkles. He carried himself precisely, almost as though unused to walking, as he moved to indicate one of my pieces on the wall. He scarcely seemed to glance at it, however, keeping his eyes firmly upon me. His eyes, like his clothing, were intensely black.

I confirmed that the work was mine and he went smoothly into his proposal. "My employer has instructed me to request your services for a particular commission."

"Your employer?" I ventured, but the question was left hanging.

"Indeed. My employer has taken an interest in your talent. He believes that you may have certain skills which might, given the right direction, be nurtured."

Suddenly I understood. This black clad stranger with his precise manner and courteous tone was a servant, a butler in all likelihood, to some wealthy individual who, unless either my ears or my instincts were failing me, wished to act as my patron! I was instantly full of questions. Who was my apparent benefactor? Where had he heard of me? Had he seen my work before? Had someone, perhaps my enthusiastic friend Horace, been spreading the good word on my behalf?

Again, I was to receive no answer. "Mr Jardine, even were I privy to my employer's private thoughts, I would not be at liberty to discuss them. I merely need to know if you will accept a special, private commission."

"Of course," I almost cried. "When?"

"Tonight."

"Tonight? But it's almost midnight already! I've been working practically since dawn."

At my protest, the servant bowed his head stiffly and strode toward the door. A few more seconds and he would be gone. There was no time to hesitate, though I may now wish that I had slammed the door at the wretched creature's back and forgot about him, his employer and the offer. But, of course, I did no such thing.

"Another time when I'm less tired," I pleaded, practically racing him for the door. "I merely worry that your employer will not get his best work when I'm so worn out!"

He paused and I think I may even have detected a smile when he said, "That is most thoughtful of you, Mr Jardine. However time is of the essence and my employer has certain requirements, which must be met. Any potential impairment in the quality of your work will, I assure you, have already been factored in. And the inconvenience to yourself has also been considered and this will reflect itself in the purse that is on offer.

"If, however, you are unable or unwilling to undertake the work at the specified time, we shall part company now and the offer will be rescinded."

"Unwilling?" I said "Not at all! Unable? I should hope not. If you will but tell me where I am expected I shall go there directly after I fetch my equipment from home."

But of this, he informed me, there was entirely no need. "All the tools of your trade are prepared and awaiting you. My employer is very particular and has certain preferences for the treatment and preparation of the canvasses he acquires and in the mixing of the paints that are used upon them. Now, if you will follow me, Mr Jardine, there is transport waiting to take you to the allotted venue."

On locking the door, I was taken aback to see a dark carriage with two black steeds between the shafts awaiting me just outside the tavern. The streets in that part of town were never busy, certainly not after dark, and I felt sure I would have heard such a vehicle pull up. But I had more on my mind than mysteries that likely didn't exist, and so I eagerly climbed aboard.

The interior was as plush as any I'd seen. Rich, red velvet cushioned the seats and curtained the windows and a comfortable journey seemed promised. Whether it was to take me near or far, I wasn't to be told, as the butler did not join me inside and the carriage sped off with me onboard alone, my mind still reeling with questions that seemed fated to go unanswered.

Such was my reverie that I lost track of time and only came to myself when the carriage slowed and finally halted. Before I could reach the handle, the door was opened and there stood that same black-eyed servant, indicating that I had reached my destination.

Beyond him, I could but dimly perceive the grey steps leading up to the rectangle of a dark door. Stepping down from the carriage, I glanced up and saw that I was being hastened toward a tall, narrow townhouse, anonymous amidst a long row of identical buildings. There was no streetlamp near enough to allow me to take in much in the way of detail, apart from the fact that no light seemed to burn within any of the rooms save the harsh yellow glow from one of the windows high above me.

Even as I observed this, I was escorted through that dark doorway. It opened onto a panelled corridor, wherein stood a woman in the traditional sombre, colourless uniform of a housekeeper. The passage was lit by the lamp she held aloft for us, which, as she stepped aside to allow us entrance, sent our shadows scampering ahead of us to be swallowed up by the gloom that lingered deeper into that house.

"Is everything in readiness?" the butler asked, as he swung the outer door closed in our wake.

The housekeeper nodded, "Mr Jardine should find everything he requires."

"In which case, you may show him to his studio." The butler then turned to me and said, "The studio is purely makeshift, until our employer is assured you will accept his sponsorship beyond this one initial sitting. However, I think you shall find it more than adequate for your needs. If you would go up now, I shall be with you presently to ensure that all is to your satisfaction." And with that, he disappeared from view, taking neither lamp nor candle as he went to whatever task awaited him in the gloomy bowels of the property.

Left alone with the housekeeper, I had little choice but to follow her up the winding staircase or else be left in the dark. The lamp's glow revealed lighter patches on the panelling where pictures had at one time hung and had never been replaced. This, coupled with the realisation that I had seen no form of furnishing or decoration save for curtains at the landing windows, did make me ponder as to what kind of art lover would own such a property. But I swiftly dismissed my concerns, reasoning that the house may have only recently been purchased, which explained the air of neglect and the chill that seemed to hang in the atmosphere.

I again tried one or two questions which had gained no answer from the butler but the housekeeper's response was the same. "I must inform you that, even were I privy to my employer's private thoughts, I would not be at liberty to discuss them." Her tone was so flat and the response so identical that I had a brief fancy that my patron's staff were practically automata, programmed with the same set of responses to any given circumstance. And, while normally I liked to pride myself on an artist's instinct in finding the essential character in the features of an individual human face, here in the shifting illumination, I found it hard to gauge anything from her neutral expression, even whether she was young or old.

We had reached the uppermost floor and I followed the rustling of her skirts as she led me along a narrow passageway with a sloping wall, toward a doorway round which a rim of bright light might be seen. Surely, before I entered that daunting studio, I could persuade her to tell me something of my assignment. "I take it that it's a portrait that's expected of me?" I allowed myself a chuckle, "Well, it'd hardly be a landscape at this time of night."

"A portrait, Mr Jardine, yes," was her only response.

"And who, may I ask, is to be my subject?"

But she merely opened the door, so that she stood as implacable as a black statue against the light beyond and, as I hesitated, intoned, "If you please, Mr Jardine, it is almost time to begin."

The long room was an attic, with a large window set into the sloping north wall and a long series of skylights in the flat roof. By day it would be filled with natural light; what better for an artist's studio? But, of course, I would be painting under starlight and the sky above me was made all the darker for the stark electrical lighting which, following my climb through murky darkness, gave off a glare of such brilliance that I almost winced.

An easel was set up in one corner by a table, upon which were arrayed brushes, charcoals, pencils, jugs of water and jars of spirits and more paint than I could have afforded after a month's bar-keeping.

However, my attention was reserved for the figure who was seated upon the large, lustrous, high-backed chair, practically a throne, at the centre of the room. The clothes of the richest fabrics, the elegantly coifed hair, the glittering, jewelled rings upon several fingers of the hands that either clasped the arm of the chair or rested upon the elaborately sculpted golden top of the ebony cane; everything about him suggested a man of noble breeding.

"Is this he? Is this my patron?" I asked the housekeeper, aware that my voice was reverently hushed as I did so. Then, all too aware that I had no idea who had brought me here, "How should I address him?"

"My instructions are that you are here to paint, not to talk.

114

You must start the painting immediately." And, indicating a bell that would summon her should I require anything, she withdrew, leaving me with my silent sitter. Suspecting that I was being put to the test and not wishing to fail at the first hurdle, I took up my pencil and, as wordlessly as the man before me, I began to draw.

Despite some effect of the lighting that seemed to leave the centre of the room in a column of vague shadow, my progress was rapid. It was a matter of moments to sketch in that classical face; broad and handsome yet, to my mind, a shade too haughty and self aware. There was arrogance there in the downward turn of the mouth. And the eyes... but the eyes were closed. Was he bored or perhaps asleep? It was, after all, now beyond midnight. Whichever it was, I was grateful for his stillness. There were no distracting movements, no sudden shifts in posture to throw out that which had already been delineated. With no idle chatter and no need to pause for the model's comfort, I was applying the broad strokes of paint before the hour was out. Indeed, my own rate of progress spurred me on and made me entirely forget how tired I had been not so long before.

Almost before I was conscious of it, I had begun picking out the details; the folds of expensive material, the ruby tie-pin, the bead of moisture on that wide, pale forehead. Had I noticed that unusual pallor previously? How could I have failed to when it stood out so starkly against the heavy blackness of the clothing and the jewels that appeared to glint so wetly? How had I missed the clamminess of the skin or the straggling limpness of the blond hair that framed that slack, blank face? Could I really have first thought him handsome and proud? There was no pride there; no thought at all.

As this realisation struck me, so too did the awareness that I had now been watching him, indeed scrutinising him in minute detail for over three hours and at no point had I seen him move. Even a sleeper makes some unconscious movements. And it was at that moment that I became suddenly aware that the portrait I was painting was that of a dead man.

\*

The artist paused in his narrative, as Drayton, seeing how unpleasant the tale was in telling, had brought him a glass of brandy. He accepted it gratefully, as did Dr Lawrence when more glasses were filled.

"A dead man," mused Lawrence, "propped up and clothed as though alive? As I recall it, in the early days of photography, families suffering bereavements frequently had a photographer make a memento of their departed loved one. One might surmise that this were a more antiquated variation on the custom, though your grim expression tells me this is too logical a theory."

Hector Jardine drained his glass and sighed, "As morbid an explanation as this would have been, it would have been preferable to the reality behind my task that night. But the truth of the matter was not to be quickly forthcoming, even after my frozen dread at being alone in the strange attic with this displayed corpse had finally thawed enough to allow me to ring for assistance."

\*

The housekeeper answered my summons so swiftly that I could easily believe she had been standing motionless in the corridor just outside the studio awaiting the bell. "May I bring you something, Mr Jardine?"

"You can get me a carriage and let me out of this madhouse," I cried, waving my hand in the direction of the ghastly seated figure. "If this is some kind of ghoulish practical joke, I want nothing to do with it! And, if it isn't, perhaps the police should be involved!"

"There is no need for such alarm, Mr Jardine." It was the butler who said so, though, apart from an odd rustling sound that I'd taken as the wind outside, I had not heard anyone enter.

"You would have me paint a cadaver's portrait and you tell me there's no need for alarm?"

"I can assure you," he soothed, "even as we speak, the person whose likeness you paint is very much alive."

"But why is he so still? Why does he look as he does?" I did not dare approach for a closer inspection but the housekeeper did, taking her lamp into that curiously lightless area. In the glow I saw that same handsome and ruddy face I had first perceived and, though it may have been but the flicker of the flame, I believed I saw movement there; a fluttering of eyelids or a trembling of the lips.

I laughed then at my ridiculous fears. I had hardly slept in twenty-four hours and, given the combination of this, the dizzying thrill of my unexpected good fortune and the curious effect of such unfamiliar lighting, perhaps my eyes had been deceiving me.

"Do not let his condition trouble you. He is quite at rest." The servant's voice was just as smooth as before and I accepted the ease and reassurance that it brought me. "Your work is proceeding admirably. Please do not let us delay you further." Then he and the housekeeper departed.

For the first time, I think, I stood back and looked at what I had thus far wrought. There was the corpse, pallid and glistening. This would not do! With fervour, I threw myself back into the portrait, determined to obliterate the hideous visage I had allowed my imaginings to impress upon my subject's own features.

My eyes must still have been adjusting to the electrical lighting, as each stroke I applied to the canvas appeared to me to shimmer and writhe. Already the sky above was paling and on and on I painted, scarcely casting a glance at the unmoving figure, allowing my hand free rein to paint what I instinctively felt was there.

The whiteness of the skin was erased, overlain by a greenish

117

grey sheen, as wet and slippery as a fish's belly. The cheeks sagged and bloated, the eyelids were puffed and purple, the mouth was merely a drooping slash across the swollen jowls from which the grey slug of a tongue threatened to topple.

The fingers that gripped the cane were distended and as fat and pale as uncooked sausages and they bulged around the corroded rings. There was a terrible wetness about him, too, that pooled out around him in a ghastly puddle. And, from this it almost seemed that a pair of sopping arms might emerge to clasp him and drag him down into impossible depths.

The blonde hair swam round the dome of the head like tendrils of bleached white seaweed. And the eyes? The eyes were finally open and they stared. But they stared sightlessly and lifelessly!

I almost fell back from the canvas when I saw what horror I had inflicted upon it. But a firm hand grasped my arm and I was propelled gently yet steadily into a chair while a glass of wine was placed into my other hand.

"Congratulations, Mr Jardine," said the butler. "You have succeeded admirably and my employer will be most satisfied."

I made to indicate the canvas but the housekeeper had already removed it from its easel and was carrying it out of the studio. Instead, I managed to gabble, "I know you think me foolish after my panic during the night but I fear that your employer may be ill." I waved my hand feebly in the direction of the still seated figure, though I did not dare look where I pointed lest there be any real resemblance to the image I had depicted.

What he replied surprised me. "Mr Jardine, you are at a misapprehension regarding the identity of your subject. Who he is need be of no concern to you. Suffice it to say that he is acquainted with my employer and that your work here tonight serves as his reward for certain deeds he has undertaken." While this was the nearest to an explanation I had received in my time there, I was loath to imagine who would want such a reward and what had been done to earn it.

The morning light had bleached the sky above us and, with a groan, I contemplated the prospect of a long day ahead of me in the public bar. But the rustle of notes in a leather wallet held out by the butler suggested that such employment might be unnecessary, for the immediate future at any rate. "You have also earned your reward," he told me, "and you will be similarly rewarded for each future commission."

Here, indeed, were riches, but the proceedings of that night had left me uneasy about accepting such strange sponsorship. I had always strived to evoke the essential beauty in life. Never before had my vision been opened up to such darkness. The words pained me but say them I must, "You may tell your employer that I must decline his patronage."

"You are in error, Mr Jardine," he said, as the housekeeper returned to stand at his shoulder. "The correct term, I believe you will find, is 'our employer'." And, as he said it, I realised for the first time that I had the wallet grasped tightly in my hand.

I sat numbly in the carriage as it drove me homeward through the now busy streets, not even bothering to part the curtains to look out at the reassuring bustle of life I heard from all around me. It seemed all too clear to me that I had accepted a deal which no sane man should ever contemplate.

And, when next I saw the face of the man I had painted that night, my estimation of his being of noble birth was confirmed. He was a lord in some coastal spot, wild in his ways, and his likeness appeared in the newspaper above a story detailing how he and a yacht loaded with his friends had been lost in a storm and dragged down into the depths of the sea.

*

"A coincidence," suggested Drayton, though his tone was more one of forlorn hope than any genuine scepticism.

Lawrence who, to my knowledge, has read much in the way of modern theory on the phenomena referred to in certain of

119

the more arcane forms of lore, wondered aloud, "Or, supposing, a case of foreknowledge. You say you painted what you 'instinctively felt'. A precognitive fugue, possibly? There are numerous accounts; a child refuses to travel on a particular train that is shortly afterwards involved in a terrible crash; someone meets a long-lost cousin out of the blue only to later find that cousin has died in a distant land."

Yet Jardine remained doubtful, shaking his head. "You see, I sensed that something else was guiding my hand. Something other. Perhaps something with no form of its own. It was there that first night and it grew stronger on each subsequent visit I was compelled to make."

"You returned? You say it as if you had no choice," put in Lawrence. "You talk of a deal, as though you had some contract. Yet you signed nothing to bind you to this patron."

"It was a sense," the artist replied. "A sinking feeling that I had somehow allowed myself to be wound up tightly in the strands of some dark web; one whose spider I could not see, yet whose presence I could feel perpetually lurking close by."

Dr Lawrence shuddered, having of late developed such an intense dislike of spiders that the mere mention of the word was practically unbearable to him. "Please, Jardine," he urged, "Continue."

"Very well," said the artist, pausing only to add, before resuming his account, "but you're wrong when you suggest I had signed no contract. I had signed something. For I always sign my work."

\*

Before the full realisation of the unnatural realm I was gradually infiltrating was upon me, however, a full day and night of sleep and a full purse did much to diminish the strangeness I had experienced, till it had only the power of a dimly remembered nightmare.

In an effort to dim these memories yet further, I worked,

making my first purchase fresh canvasses. I had, for months, been painting and repainting on the same frames, each new piece obliterating an earlier work. But no more! I had canvasses and paint and the luxury of time to devote to them. I was as happy as ever my friends had seen me. "As cheerful as a lad who's got back from playing truant to discover the school's ablaze," was how Horace put it, reasoning, "That can only mean you've been playing host to the muse. If you have anything ready, I may have an empty space on one of my walls."

I showed him one painting, then two, then a dozen. "These are extraordinary!" he exclaimed, "The vibrancy! You might almost smell the blossom in this meadow or hear the rustling of the grass in this view of the park," and more such flattery that it would do me no service to repeat. But I will repeat his criticism, "There are no figures to give them a sense of place or scale. But I would certainly consider any one or two of these when they're ready."

And, when they were ready, Horace was as good as his word and they were exhibited. Though I had held back my own words, unable to tell him what had brought about my change in fortune and what also stayed my hand from capturing the images of the people who should, by rights, have been populating my landscapes.

It was as they were hanging in this very gallery that I met Margaruite, the young woman who might have been... no, who was, outside of painting, the one love of my life. And the one love that did not turn on me!

She had, in my hearing, praised the lifelike quality of a group of children whom I had included indulging in a game of chase in the woods on the edge of the park. When her companion, the elderly dragon to whom, I later discovered, she was secretary, companion and, it seemed, general skivvy, had moved out of earshot, I gently told this enchanting young lady that they were no more real than the cherubs in a churchyard.

"And how would you know," she retorted, unwilling to

encourage this lunatic who accosted women in art galleries, "unless you were there when the picture was painted?"

"Oh, I was there all right and I know that these children, in fact every last person depicted here, exists only in the mind of the artist; he being me."

This seemed to delight her and she was radiant when delighted. "You painted this? And that one, also? And you're not lying to try and turn the head of a country girl new to the city? And all of these people came out of your imagination?"

I told her, "There are many things lurking in my imagination," and I even managed to smile as I said it.

Horace, I know, remembers Margaruite well since, from that point, she was a frequent visitor to the gallery and, later to my studio. She also painted; vivid, bold, colourful pieces, full of a vitality that I envied. But she would let no-one see them but myself. Horace will also remember how we laughed and talked and how she encouraged my every effort and the plans we had. Such plans!

Then, one night, as I made my way back from a long session in the studio transferring that day's sketches of a country lake to canvas, there, in the street where I lived, a black carriage was waiting.

So many months had passed since that strange night that, after an initial cold jolt on seeing the vehicle, I became convinced that its presence there was a coincidence and it had no connection to my prior experience and I hurried past it to the safety of home.

The sight of the butler waiting on the steps of my building proved me sadly wrong and, as he took a pocket watch from the folds of his black waistcoat, I knew that midnight must be close at hand.

As the carriage sped on, with me yet again alone inside, it did occur to me to attempt discovering something of my destination. But, when I parted the curtains I found darkly frosted windows that stubbornly refused to be budged. All my scrabblings were for nothing and, when the butler once more opened the door, he glanced at the glass with glittering eyes that appeared aware of my attempts.

Under the moon that glowered down on us that night, the townhouse looked gaunt and decayed and once I was again in the care of the housekeeper I noted, by her lamp's light, that the banisters and the corners were thickly coated in dust and hung heavy with cobwebs. I swear I even saw strands of the stuff within the dark pleats of that woman's dress and amongst the tresses of her hair; as if, since last I had seen her, she had somehow remained still and frozen into position, dutifully awaiting my next appointment at that skulking property.

The studio was as before, but with fresh canvas on the easel and fresh paints on the table. And, naturally, a fresh subject in the chair. On this night it was a woman; one who, with her features skilfully accentuated by cosmetics and her perfectly presented face framed by silken, shimmering hair, should almost certainly have been beautiful had there been any spark of life about her. Yet she sat as still and as rigid as the drowned lord.

Did I even think to run, as I should have? No! I stayed and I painted and as I did, the sensation grew in me that not only was this woman dead but, if I did dare approach her and lay a hand on her cold flesh, there would be nobody there at all, just the dispersing shadow of an image projected from some distant source.

But I did not approach her and, after a while, I did not even see her. And, by dawn, I had a completed portrait of a corrupted hag; her decaying flesh streaked and daubed by powder and make-up that did little to conceal the ugliness etched in every line and turned her into a grotesque parody, a mummified circus clown. And her neck, which twisted at an angle no neck should ever twist at, was bare and bony, since that long and shining hair of hers had been pulled back sharply from her head; clawed by what appeared to be a branch, but which might have been a shrivelled arm with its stick-like fingers so enmeshed in her hair that she dangled limply from it.

And her eyes? They bulged piteously in horror, shock and a final, ghastly realisation that I was glad I could not share.

"What kind of reward is this?" I demanded of the butler, as the canvas was once again spirited away.

"A reward for vanity," he suggested, "providing, in art, a mirror that shows only the truth within? Would such an answer relieve your turmoil? But why should such matters trouble you, Mr Jardine? What you paint is simply the truth, even if those it portrays cannot yet see it. But they will, in the fullness of time."

Then he gave me my money and I accepted it and I was driven home, where I slept and I arose and I painted bright, hopeful scenes and I made my plans with Margaruite and I never once told her of my nocturnal occupation.

It was at this time, when my days were filled with such happiness and success, that I was called for most frequently by night. Eventually the butler did not even appear and I simply climbed aboard the carriage when I found it waiting for me. By this stage I'd already stopped accepting the wages my employer arranged for me after each visit.

I cannot tell you how many of these portraits I undertook. I had contemplated arming myself with a flask of alcohol to help blot out the faces before me but, the worst of it is, I didn't even need it. I had become an expert, you see, at not recognising those put up for my attentions as people. They were objects to be detailed and that was all. But, traces still remain, even now.

Some of these faces, or faces that seemed familiar to me, I saw again in reports of tragedy, horror, execution and death. Always death! Here was the murderess, found broken-necked, hanged by her own hair; the thief entombed and asphyxiated in the vault he chose to rob; the huntsman savaged by his own dogs or worse; the drowned lord's debaucheries drifting slowly to light... It troubled me less when the person seated in that chair was old and in the twilight of their life but, at least once, I think there may have been a child!

My other life, that which was lived in daylight, was as

successful as it had ever been. My work was exhibiting and selling. I was the consummate showman, unveiling masterpiece after masterpiece, triumph after triumph and I was fêted and befriended by all, it seemed. I had even persuaded Margaruite to show Horace some of her paintings. And when she announced, "He actually likes them," she appeared to find the notion preposterous, exciting and terrifying all at the same time. "He wants to put them in his next show. I'll be next to you!"

"Where you belong, always," I told her.

"I couldn't be prouder," she smiled. "You know how I adore your work; how you can capture the mood of a moment and how the people in them all appear so alive." And she was still smiling when she said the last words I would ever have wanted to hear. "You should paint portraits! I wish you would! I wish you would paint me and make me look as alive as your other paintings."

The horror in my face was plain to see and the effect was instantly wounding to that poor girl who could have had no idea of the thoughts that screamed in my mind. She was hurt, then angry, then confused and, all the time, I was thinking furiously. I swear, I even contemplated thrusting my hand into the fire to give me a way out of this impossible task. Would that I'd had the courage!

But, my rational mind protested, I was my own man and this was no commission. And hadn't there been something about the mixing of the paints and the preparation of the canvas for those sponsored paintings; some glamour, might you call it, in those instruments that affected the portrait produced? And I would use normal paints and regular canvas, paid for from my own earnings not from my patron's purse. And I would not be painting by midnight. And as a fool can easily persuade himself of anything if he tries hard enough, I agreed.

"May I move now? Is it finished?" Margaruite had scarcely been able to sit still during that long afternoon. And, when I told her I was done, she leapt forward, crying, "I must see!"

125

"Please," I tried to hold her back, too exhausted to be effective against her joyful enthusiasm. "Margaruite, please don't!"

"Oh." The sound, as she made it, was so hollow I would have wept if I'd had the strength. Then, when she turned from the canvas to me, there was a glimmer in her eyes and an edge in her voice I had never known before. "Is this some strange form of joke, Hector?"

"I'm sorry," I mumbled, "I'm sorry I can't explain... What I see when I look at you..."

"This is what you see when you look at me?" She dragged me over to the canvas, making me look at what those dreadful hours had achieved. "You see nothing?"

"No..." How could I tell her? What could I say?

She was crying now, pointing at the dull emptiness of the canvas. "You see nothing when you look at me? Because there's nothing there! The canvas is blank!"

I cannot tell you what I saw when Margaruite posed for me that day. The memory is buried away in such a deep and dark place that I will not even approach it. But I couldn't put it down on the canvas. I had tried to paint the warm and smiling face that was in my memory, but something else kept forcing its way to the surface, so overwhelming in its intensity that I could only allow my hand to trace it in the air rather than preserve it on the canvas.

Margaruite looked bewildered as I slumped before her, as vacant as the portrait I had failed to paint. "Is it something I've done? Are you trying to tell me something?"

No, I thought! Not done... not done yet!

"Why are you shaking so?" There was fear now in her voice, anger softening into concern. "You've been so distracted these past few days. Are you ill? What's wrong?"

"Go!" I yelled it. "For God's sake, Margaruite, just go!"

I could see that she didn't understand but I could do nothing to make her understand. And, even if I had, what I had done on those ghastly night sittings would surely have damned me in

126

her eyes! "I cannot look at you! Please, go!"

That was the last time she and I ever saw one another. Call me a coward if you will, but how could I spend my days and nights with her when I had seen what I had seen? When I knew how her days would end?

The carriage came for me that night but, this on this occasion, it was I that awaited its approach. The butler had taken the journey with it. And, just this one time, he sat with me inside as the waiting house beckoned.

"I thought it was the paints," I protested. "Something in the preparations..."

"Ah, but once you have worked with them and mastered the technique you may have found yourself possessed of talents you had never utilised before," said he. "After all, while the artist has a clear effect on the medium, perhaps the medium may also have its own effect on the artist."

"Then I'll have no more of it! My commission ends now!"

"Of course, Mr Jardine," he agreed, stepping out of the carriage before that decomposing townhouse. "No-one has compelled you to remain under our employer's patronage. But there is the matter of tonight's appointment and I gravely doubt you would wish to miss the chance to paint the one responsible for your recent experiences."

And so I followed that stiffly moving housekeeper, with her lamp that no longer worked and her face so veiled in webs that she wouldn't have noticed anyway; up those steps and into the studio to finally encounter the monster that dwelled within.

After that night, the black carriage has not come back.

I forced myself not to run back to Margaruite and, when she left to return to her hometown, I no longer had the agonising pleasure of watching her from afar while trying desperately to convince myself that I could forget what I had seen and that the knowledge would not pray on us both until I had to share it rather than go mad. I still hope that I was wrong and that what I thought I saw was no more than the projection of my own terrors. But what if my own terrors are what shaped events for all I painted? I pray not. And I hope she is happy and her life without me has been a good one.

My own life has been a struggle since then. Horace was right; the paintings needed figures. But there are no figures in the park at twilight or dusk. For these are the only times I feel it is safe to paint, lest a memory of a passer-by become part of the composition and some hellish fate make itself apparent.

Yet, still, I paint. But only I see the results. They are not for exhibition. I do not display my work anymore.

Not until now…

\*

All eyes turned to the silk-draped square on the wall. The artist's story seemed at an end but the very presence of this object was itself the subject of a mystery that only Horace Drayton could put to rest. It was Lawrence who posed the question. "Where and how, exactly, did you find this picture?"

"That's just the damnedest thing," Drayton pondered, furrowing his brow. "For I didn't so much find it as…"

"It found you," supplied Lawrence, this almost seeming to confirm a suspicion he had been entertaining. "And, through you, it found Jardine. But how was it brought into your orbit?"

"A woman," said Drayton, hollowly. "A stiff, strangely spoken woman. She said her… her employer had instructed her to dispose of it and she was to take any price for it and perhaps it might be particularly rewarding to one of my visitors. Then she was gone. A servant, I thought, from some wealthy family, for she was met at the door by a man in butler's uniform and carried off in a massive black carriage. You see, this is how I know Hector's story to be true. And… as she climbed into the carriage, I thought I saw some other within; a darker shape within the red, velvet darkness. A shape that seemed to smile."

"Could he have been here?" murmured Lawrence in horrified excitement.

*The Crimson Picture*

But there was to be no answer as, with a halting step, Jardine had moved to the shrouded painting. Then, with the lingering traces of a showman's instinct, he grasped the silk and, with a cry of, "They brought it here to be exhibited? Then let us look on it one last time. Let us all look upon the face of the monster," he tore the covering away.

When he told me of his experience, Dr Lawrence still found it hard to put into words what he saw depicted on that crimson canvas, but the impression he gave was of something bellowing, insane and infernal. He spoke of those clawed hands that gripped the arms of the throne with such force that the wood should surely splinter. He said something of a gaping chasm of a mouth that seemed to shriek its silent madness into the air around the painting, so that it shimmered like a heat haze of hellish intensity. He also made mention of the veins and arteries that stood out tense on practically every inch of exposed flesh and that appeared to pulse with livid ferocity.

And, finally, he whispered of the eyes. And, as he did so, his face was ashen and there was a tremor in his voice. "Those staring, maddened, baleful eyes that saw everything! A gaze that appeared to find me and crawl all over me like..." and here he had to force the words past his lips, "like thin-legged red spiders! It held me, almost seeing within me. Into the heart of who I am. Into my very soul! And these eyes saw so much more than eyes are meant to see that they were bleeding wet, red tears."

"This is your work?" Lawrence demanded, looking at the artist with a mixture of pity, chilling horror and, hard to credit, fascinated admiration. He could scarcely believe that the painting before him was the work of this gentle man, or of any man. "But it's unsigned. You said you always sign your work."

"It is signed," Jardine moaned softly, "I had forgotten... forced the memory from my mind, just as I had done with all those blank, oblivious faces, but I remember it now that I see it with my own eyes. There! Signed by my hand... but the signature is the artist's own!" And as he slumped back into his

129

seat, he pointed a shaking hand toward the lower corner of the canvas. There, a symbol, almost like a coat of arms, appeared to be etched into the arm of the throne beneath the monstrous subject's left hand; and was that the shadow of some other, yet more ghastly hand, that seemed to lurk there?

Lawrence dropped his glass, numbed by the full significance of what he was seeing. "You said something else guided your hand. Something with no form of its own, working through you!"

"What does it mean?" urged Drayton, still squinting at the symbol, which appeared to him to be an arch or gateway framing a bestial form; possibly a goat but, more likely, a satyr or hobgoblin. "Whose insignia is this?"

Dr Lawrence, who had encountered a similar symbol with alarming regularity in some of his less orthodox studies, had his suspicions but, whether or not he would have risked sharing them even he doesn't know. For, at that instant, there was an agonised grunt from Jardine, who had flung himself rigid in his chair.

"It's the strain of telling that ghastly story again," cried Drayton, rushing to his friend. "I should never have asked him! We must do something!"

But, with a final spasm and a noise that might have grown to a scream if there had been air to power it, there was nothing any human agency could do for Hector Jardine. The boy, Ernest, having heard the commotion, was sent to fetch a doctor. All Lawrence could do was assure his former school friend that Jardine had seemed relieved in the telling of the tale and the sharing of his private burden.

When the doctor was done, his first diagnosis, though it would have to be later verified through post-mortem procedures, was that Hector Jardine had died, almost instantaneously, from a brain haemorrhage. And, as the pronouncement was made, Lawrence could not help but think on such a death, the crimson fluid filling the brain, enveloping it and drowning it. And, as he experienced this image, he turned his eyes between the crimson picture and the mortal remains of the painter; his eyes wide and staring, his mouth gaping, his hands clutching so tightly that the doctor struggled to prise the clawing fingers away from the arms of the chair. And, in that instant, he saw that this indeed was the work of the artist's own hand, a final self-portrait.

When the artist had been removed and the portrait covered once more, the two former school friends sat sharing a silence, until Drayton murmured, "She is alive, you know. Margaruite, I mean. But I think I know what Hector saw. She had an accident, you see, after they had parted. That's why she went back home, where there was someone to care for her while she adapted to her condition. For she's blind.

"She has learned to cope with it admirably. She was always strong in spirit. But for Hector, a man who lived by his sight more fully than any of his other senses, can there have been a more horrible fate for him to await for a loved one?"

"Maybe not," Lawrence agreed, "but given what his eyes had witnessed, might there not also have been a degree of jealousy amidst the horror?"

All that remains to be said is that, though Jardine is dead and the portrait burned, there are frequently works by centuries-dead artists found mouldering away in their hiding places and long forgotten vaults. As Lawrence somewhat worriedly expressed his thoughts on the matter, "Who knows when any of us might find ourselves in some unknown gallery in some unfamiliar place and what face we might discover in a dark and dusty canvas, staring back at us with all too familiar eyes?"

# SQUABBLE

## D. F. Lewis

I opened the stop-gap as far as it would go, to cope with the grinding and grating symptoms – and, being the night watchman on duty, I was the only one there to cope with the rust-corroded screw-hole.

However, I was pleased to see that, one after another, the previously disused pistons gradually rose from the beds, tumblers clicked into place with a musical unison and, finally, I felt the deep-gutted rhythms vibrating up the handle upon which I still clung with dear life.

But, then, abruptly, a little girl materialised. I suspect she must have been hiding behind one of the studded tanks, which had just erupted into gurgling, rasping life. The first thought was that this was a stowaway who had been gently, innocently slumbering, only to be rudely awoken by my tussle with the cranking cocks.

"Who art thou?" I tried to sound comforting, but there was no reply.

By now, the machinery was returning to an even keel, humming sweetly, just as if it had been oiling along forever. I could now evidently release the shaft-stop since, without my continuing intervention, it could no doubt find its own pecking order in the scheme of the moving parts.

I wondered why all this trouble had to happen on *my* night of caretaking. It should have happened to rogues such as Billy Belly, Paddy Weggs or Feemy Fitzworth… or to that Fred Tyrell who nobody liked…

I turned to the little girl and motioned her to sit by me while I kept an eye on the dials, which, after several minutes of violent fluctuations either side of norm, were now easing back from the over-generous tolerances into more acceptable margins of error.

"Well, what dost thou think thou art doing hiding back

132

there, little girlie? That there tank could've back-spurted some pretty nasty gooey stuff into thy winsome hair and scalded thy comely petal cheeks."

The little girl touched her large-looped ribbon at the back of her head to check it was still in place, and then felt towards the clipped-back hair at the temples to ensure not a single strand had escaped. Feeling satisfied with her demeanour, she was able to reply.

"I always hide back there to get away from t'other children."

"And why, my dear, may I ask, art thou so afrit of t'other children?"

"They make fun of me, say I'm old-fashioned, say I've got a big spamhead, laugh at my pink hair-ribbon, say I read books too much, say I'm weird, say I'm ill-bred, say I'm..."

"Hold on, hold on. A pretty little lady like thee, with such generous depths to the eyes, this won't do, this won't do at all. Children are so cruel to each other. Tell me what thy name is, and I'll see what I can do for thee."

"Pansy."

"Pansy what, may I ask, dumpling?"

"Pansy..." she hesitated, "...Tyrell."

I recalled her father, Fred, whom nobody liked, and everything clicked into place. No wonder the other children called her names. But sticks and stones...

On impulse, I picked her up like a rag doll and, not even with a farewell hug, plunged her into a section of the mechanical workings. This, so that the flesh and bone of her tiny body could act as the grease and washer on a piston-system which was fast grinding to a halt in a new spite of gremlins, caused – I guessed – by a bad dose of bald torque in one of the clogging cogs and chronic ingrowth of friction in the central pump-head.

After a series of juddering false starts, the skewed fly-wheels meshed on bone-marrow, with one mere spray of skull shards spat out from various interfaces and a single dollop of creamy-red backwash in the overflow bilge.

## Squabble

When Fred Tyrell arrived to relieve me as night watchman, I exchanged a surly greeting with him, allowing the earlier squabble and ill-feeling between us to be buried at last... then left for bed. There didn't seem any point for much else. The machine was once again humming sweetly.

# THE EYE IN THE MIRROR

## Eddy C. Bertin

Frank Hellinger enjoyed his private thoughts, walking home on that sweet summer evening. It had been one of those rare really beautiful days with the afternoon sun bathing your body in its warmth and gently heating your face, then with the evening slowly falling a soft sweet breeze caressing your temples. Frank loved it, it had been a lovely day and now it was a perfect evening for a murder.

He had been enjoying the idea and the details for the whole of the long walk back from the pub, which was some three miles away from his home. In as far as he could still think of it as home whilst Liz was there. He cherished the idea of finally putting an end to it all, stopping the constant infernal nagging, ending the continual bitching, silencing her once and for all. With increasing frequency, he had wanted to hit her, felt a desire to smash his fist into that blabbering shrieking mouth, but that sort of vulgar violence was not for him. The last months and weeks and days he'd often wondered why it hadn't come to this sooner. The final result was inevitable. After all, what's so special about a murder? You only have to work out all the details carefully in advance, don't stray from the plan, make no mistakes, overlook no details, foresee all possible complications that might get in the way. It's really not that difficult, he thought. Just read the newspapers. People are murdered every day, for the stupidest things. Like sticking your finger out of the window of your car at some geek on a motorcycle. A motorcycling geek who just happens to have a gun in his pocket. Or just being at the wrong checkout in the supermarket at the wrong time. The time when a junkie decides that now's the time to get the money for his next fix. Stupid murders without any finesse, created on the spur of the moment.

Such murders were so crude, so senseless, they insulted his

135

intelligence.

He arrived at his home, and as always enjoyed the sight of the lonely house. It was a Victorian style house, built right in the middle of the woods, isolated, but yet only a few miles from the next village, with its shops and pub. It had seemed so perfect to them when they were first married. But then, everything had seemed perfect with Liz being pregnant and them being so in love. Till the baby was born dead and everything changed in the years that followed. Not a chance of another child, and the bitterness inside her had grown and grown until it turned on to him.

He opened the door and before he had the chance to close it behind him his wife called out from the kitchen: "Don't slam the fucking door!"

Frank smiled. "No, dear," he said and closed the door gently.

He took off his coat and put it on the hat-stand. In doing so he put his foot against the umbrella-holder which fell over with a loud clang. He bent to pick it up.

"What did you knock over now, you clumsy idiot?" Liz yelled.

"Why nothing, dear," he said gently, "nothing at all of importance."

"That's not what I heard," she replied, "and don't you dear me, you're late again. I suppose you've been in that pub again?"

"Yes dear," Frank sighed, "I have indeed." He had long since given up lying about such matters.

He righted the umbrella-holder, and took a cigarette from the porcelain box on the hall cupboard. He took his lighter and flicked it.

"And don't you dare smoke again before dinner. How often do I have to tell you? You'll have bad breath the whole evening and won't be able to taste a thing as it should. Not that you will with what you've no doubt drunk already."

"Right, dear," Frank said, putting the unlit cigarette back.

His wife came in to the hall, her hair dangling before her eyes. "That bloody stupid hair-dresser," she said, "never can get it how I want it."

"You look lovely as usual, my dear," Frank said.

She shrugged. "Dinner will be ready in a few minutes," she said, "and don't you try to get another drink before, Frank, I'm warning you."

Liz turned to go back to the kitchen.

"Don't worry, I won't," Frank said.

He opened the upper drawer of the cupboard, took out the transparent plastic rain coat and put it over his head. Putting on the thin surgical gloves took only a second. He smiled and went after his wife. Oh, it all went so smoothly, he had practised it all, it only needed a few seconds, she hadn't even left the hall.

The knife came out of his pocket as if of its own accord; it was one of the steak knives from the kitchen. One moment his fingers had been stroking it, and then suddenly it was in his hand, solid and cold. Two quick steps and he was behind her; his left arm came up and closed like a snake around her throat, blocking whatever sounds she was going to make. He pulled her back towards him, as his right hand holding the knife plunged the blade into her.

Time froze as he held it there for an instant. In the hall mirror in front of her he saw her face, her mouth opening wide into a gasping hole from which not a sound emerged, her eyes staring at their reflection in the mirror, a loving couple embracing. Her hands fluttered aimlessly in the air like lost butterflies.

She didn't realise, she didn't realise at all what was happening, what he was doing, oh, wasn't this marvellous? He pulled the knife free and plunged it in again, a bit higher, below her shoulder blades. It went in deep. He felt it grate against a rib for a moment, twisted it a bit and felt it sinking in her flesh and innards. He put all his weight and strength on the blade, plunging it into her body like a sacrificial spear, a cold penis of deadly steel.

She began trembling, suddenly she hiccoughed and blood spurted from her mouth and down her dress. She coughed, more blood, then her eyes rolled and turned white.

He withdrew the knife and took a step back, letting her loose. For a second she stood upright, on shaking legs, then she just crumpled and fell down.

That's it? He thought. Curiously he looked down at the bloodied knife in his plastic covered hand. The rain coat had been superfluous, no blood on it at all. Well, it hadn't cost much anyway.

Frank looked down at the motionless body in the hall.

"Liz?" he asked, "Lizzie, dear?"

The body didn't move, but he plunged the knife in again for good measure. In a way he felt a bit disappointed. All those weeks and months of thinking it all out, reliving in advance what happened now, and it had all seemed so much more exciting than... just this. You put a knife in her back, and she just runs down and stops, and that's it. Pretty boring, but of course that was all it was. No drums, no fanfare, no applause, just a sudden silence enveloping the hall and the house. No more "Dear, don't", no more... just nothing at all. He had done it at last; he had killed her.

He had never felt so relaxed in his whole life. He went to the kitchen, tore open the drawer and scattered the other knives and forks and such on the floor. He poured himself a straight bourbon from the bar, and sipped it slowly as he thought everything over.

Drink finished, he rinsed the glass and put it back in its place. Then he overturned the small bar, crashing bottles and glasses all over the floor. The strong smell of spilled alcohol mingled with the slightly sweet odour of fresh blood. That was still running out of her open mouth, turning her teeth red, and now a smaller stream spread from under her back.

Frank went through the house, opening drawers and

throwing stuff around: papers, clothes, underwear. It will take me some time to clean up this mess, he thought.

He took Liz's jewels, put them in his pocket, and smashed the box against the wall. He went out and dumped them in the nearby river. He felt a tinge of regret about discarding the jewels, they were after all worth a lot of money, but he couldn't risk hiding them somewhere.

Then he went back home, and used a crowbar to force open the door.

He went inside his burgled house, found his murdered wife and finally phoned the police.

They asked all the questions he knew they would ask, but Frank was prepared for them. He stuck to his 'story' rather than coming up with a complicated alibi:

While he was out walking, and yes, visiting the pub, a burglar had obviously entered the house. There had been a confrontation. His wife was hot-headed and would've been furious at the intrusion. There had been a fight and the burglar had got hold of a knife and stabbed her. It was as simple as that.

Frank went willingly with them to the police station, exhibiting the expected quota of shock and grief. Not too much grief, though – being in shock he was still unable to comprehend the fact fully that his wife was really dead, stabbed for a bunch of not so very expensive jewels which had been taken. He was surprised that they cross-examined him for what seemed an eternity. Not that he was the slightest bit worried, not even when they said he had to spend the night in a cell and reminded him of his right to call a lawyer. What the fuck? he said, I don't need a lawyer. They seemed to think otherwise, fuck them.

Frank slept amazingly well in his cell, and awoke feeling better than he ever had since marrying Liz. He started thinking about lawyers, they were no problem, with Liz dead he had money to burn. They'd get him out of here in no time, but still requiring the assistance of a lawyer would make him look suspicious. So when they asked him again if he wanted to make a phone call, he declined, playing the husband who after a night behind bars has suddenly realised that his wife really has been murdered.

They had nothing on him, he thought, not a single shred of real evidence, not even any fingerprints. All his friends would testify, if necessary, that he and Liz had a model marriage, that they never quarrelled... Thank Liz for that, when she was bitching at him she had at least always done it in private, with no witnesses around. The glorified image of her happy marriage had been holy to her. Bless her soul!

He started suspecting something was wrong when they came for him after breakfast and he was back in the cold grey interrogation room, in the presence of a creepy looking character. The guy had a nose hooked like an eagle's beak and deep eyes that kept on shifting; he looked like a character straight out of an old EC comic. He also had a small black suitcase from which he took a set of photographs which he spread on the table in front of Frank, without saying a word.

Frank took a look at the pictures and gasped. The pictures were weird, slightly blurred at the edges, and the centre was circular, as if taken through a bizarre camera lens. Still, they clearly showed some things he really didn't like. The photographs were frontally taken. He saw his wife's face, looking straight into the eye of the camera, and himself behind her, his one arm circling her throat, the other behind her back. Then came more photographs, showing him as he stepped back, the bloodied knife in his hand, and then plunging it in again, straight into her back. The image was tilting on those photographs as his wife was sliding down.

He stared at the men around him, observing him coldly. The creep character was grinning, showing his bad yellowed teeth; the fucking creep was practically drooling.

"This is some kind of sick joke," Frank whispered roughly. "This is a shameless forgery, it can't be..."

"Oh yes, it can."

They grinned at him.

"You see what she saw in the mirror, in front of her as she was murdered. It's retina photography... We've been experimenting with it for some time, but it's not something we crow about in public yet. Sometimes it works, when the murder victim gets a good look at their murderer at the instant of death. Death petrifies those last images in several layers on her retina, petrified witnesses. The last images, and if we are quick enough we can save them, recreate them."

Frank dashed the pictures from the table, unable to stop himself. "This is insane," he yelled, "my wife didn't get a look at..."

Mr Creep and his colleagues looked at each other, then back at him, benign smiles on their lips.

"Your wife didn't get *what*, Mr Hellinger? You were going to say she didn't get a look at her murderer, weren't you? But as you can see, you're quite mistaken. She got a bloody good look at him, she was looking straight in the mirror, an eye in the mirror staring at you, when you stabbed her twice in the back."

Mr Creep bent down and started picking up the scattered photographs.

"I want a lawyer," Frank stammered. "This insane stuff, it will never hold up in court."

But of course it did.


The verdict fell six months later, when Frank went to trial. They had dredged in the river and found the missing jewels. The jury's verdict was murder in the first degree, the death penalty. Frank's lawyer went to a higher court, which after some more months confirmed the original sentence.

Seventeen months after he had murdered his wife, Frank Hellinger woke on a chilly morning, shivering after another night full of dreadful nightmares. But the real nightmare started when the white-suited men came into his cell and took him, kicking and screaming, and cursing the priest who just stood around and watched since his sympathy wasn't wanted. In the other cells some early risers were making a noise, yelling, banging things against the bars as Frank was escorted to the place of execution. But most didn't care, just another one on his way.

"I don't want to, I don't want to," he shrieked as they bound him on the bed in the windowless room. Not even a glimmer of early sunlight, never to see dawn again, never again being able to walk and speak. The fear nearly drove him insane, his mind was shrieking like a crazy rabbit in his skull. They said some things, but he didn't hear what. He had been preparing for this moment for weeks, but it hadn't been enough.

He wet himself when they plunged the needle into his vein, a cold sparkling finger of death. He twisted and turned, his mouth foaming. He cursed his executioners, even cursed himself. He felt the poison start its course through his body, his stomach cramped, he wanted to kick the poison out. His tongue swelled, hung out of his dry lips, he bit it and tasted the last thing in life, his own blood. His short fingernails scratched the bed, and then the poison reached his heart and his body went limp, his brain plunged his shrieking mind into total and final darkness.

He awoke with a metallic buzzing in his ears, something that could be a voice, or a swarm of irritating bees. Unbelieving he opened his eyes and closed them again when dazzling white light burned into them.

He felt his heart thumping in his ears, his tongue a dry slug in his mouth, his body stiff and painful.

Hell. I'm in Hell, he thought. And opened his eyes very slowly.

White walls around him, a bed or something on which he was lying. Frank sat up. His legs and arms felt stiff, as if he hadn't moved them for some time. He licked his lips, grateful for the bit of saliva. I'm dead, he told himself, I'm dead yet… I live?

He was sitting on the couch in his own room, in his own house. He felt something against his skin and touched his head. He felt some kind of electric cable and rubbery things attached to his head. He tore them loose and let them drop. He heard them fall, what a blessed sound!

His fingers caressed the couch; he let them crawl over his face, his nose, his mouth. Alive, he was fucking alive!

Then he saw the small electronic device resting on the table, next to the couch on which he had been lying.

Which was where the buzzing sound came from, only now his mind recognised it as a voice. Metallic, artificial, but yet very real.

"Hello, Mr Hellinger," the voice rasped. "Please stay seated, remain calm and just listen. We know that some of our customers have trouble adjusting after a session, which is why this tape is prepared to start as soon as you wake up."

Session? Wake up? What was going on? Bloody hell! He had murdered his wife and in turn been executed for his crime. Yet... he took a deep breath, smelled the slightly dusky air of the room. He moved his hands and fingers, felt his body. No, he was not dead!

"We are Therapeutics Limited," the voice from the device continued, "your very own private psychiatrist, and you have been undergoing a very specific therapeutic session of your own free will. It may be confusing right now, but you will soon recall all the details. You came to us when you discovered some severely hostile tendencies in your behaviour which you wanted cured. Our speciality is that we are *extremely* private: the session and the cure are strictly between you and the therapy machine. You were linked to the therapy machine which probed into your problems, as you gave it freedom to do. Everything is strictly between yourself and the machine; the machine is not linked to anyone else, not even to us. After the initial session, the computer developed the ideal curing session for your specific problem, which I repeat, we as developers are unaware of and will never know of. The treatment you have been undergoing, involved self-hypnosis and sub-ego therapy. It is the principle of a mind cleaning itself; your own mind getting rid of all its problems. The time needed for the session depends on the problems, but in most cases this will not have been more than a few hours. You are awake now, and you are cured. Your mind has cured itself. That is our total guarantee. The session has been recorded for your own convenience; you can make a copy from the hard disk if you desire to do so. You are by now aware of what has happened: you have put yourself under treatment. This has been successful, as we guaranteed. You may now disconnect from the machine, if you have not already done so. If you do not want to keep a copy of the session, just push the red button on the machine, and all information will be erased forever. This of course is part of the total privacy policy you subscribed to."

Frank shook his head, he had a bit of a headache, but otherwise felt just fine. He remembered. Oh yes, he remembered now! A cure, that was all it had been... He now remembered the ads for self cure through Therapeutics Ltd. A highly respected firm, and highly bloody expensive too, but yes, it had been worth it. Though he still wondered why he had chosen this solution, his mind wasn't yet working at full speed. He remembered the sales pitch: the machine created the dark fantasies in his own mind, explored his psychosis and made him work it out, then made his mind face the consequences. Quite nasty, in fact, but this way it should be out of his system.

He erased the hard disc of the computer, disconnected the machine. So small and yet so powerful, it had all seemed so bloody real, but of course that was what it was intended to be.

His head was clearing now, the last cloudy whispers going away from his thoughts. He remembered having to pay the full treatment fee in advance, and on top of that a deposit for the machine. In cash, no credit cards. Tomorrow he would take the machine back to Therapeutics Ltd, and get his deposit back.

As he took a few steps, the room swayed around him. A feeling of unreality engulfed Frank and he grabbed hold of the couch to steady himself. For a moment he had the weirdest idea that his hands were sinking through the couch, sinking through reality and ending up... where?

The feeling passed; he took a deep breath. The memories of the nightmare he had been going through those last months still seemed so very real, though the session must have taken no more than... A few hours? He looked at his watch, but had no idea when the session had started. Flashes of the nightmare still lingered in his mind. He still felt his arm circling around Liz, and the way he had plunged the knife in her back, and then again harder and more upwards. His mind really had put him in front of a dark mirror. He still saw Mr Creep's face when he displayed the retina photographs, he remembered the months in prison, he still felt the cold needle slipping death into his veins. Well, it was over now. He had done the best thing, he had cured himself before he did something from which there was no turning back. Or had he? Why then still those weird flashes, those memories of what had never happened?

He found Liz lying on the floor. She was face down, in front of the mirror, her back a red-splattered mess. The blood had dried and turned a dark brown; a few flies were swarming around her body. The handle of the knife was sticking out of her back, like an accusing penis.

His heart stopped for a moment. His eyes wandered around the room, seeing the overturned furniture, the smashed bottle and glasses.

The cure had been very effective. But a bit too late.

Oh yes, he remembered now. The final test.

Flashes of the nightmare came back, whispering in his mind. The men grinning at him, Mr Creep with his retina photographs, the long months in jail, the trials, the final needle. He saw his own white distorted face in the mirror, the last

145

thing Liz had seen.

Frank Hellinger grinned. Oh yes, the cure had been a good idea after all. Though he had used it too late for Liz, but in good time for him.

Who the hell had ever heard of retina photographs? Frank shook his head in disbelief. Cure myself? Fuck that, he thought. The deed was already done when I underwent the 'cure'. And he had undergone that merely to see what eventualities he may have overlooked. Oh, wasn't that a smart idea?

He went over to Liz's body, felt her skin. Nice and cold. He checked and saw that her jewels were gone, so was the plastic coat. Good, he thought, I only forgot the knife. That won't take long.

He turned her body over. Blood had scrawled spider webs under her. As he had feared, her eyes were wide open, staring at him even in death.

Oh no, dear, it won't work this time, Frank thought. He wrapped his fingers in a handkerchief, took the handle of the knife and with some effort pulled it out. Fresh blood began to run.

He looked down at her, smiled and lifted the knife. Then plunged it down. Once, twice. Bye bye retinas.

Quite messy. But quite effective.

Then he went out to get rid of the knife. He'd go for a nice walk; after all it was a beautiful evening, and stop by the pub for a drink or two. Then he would come home, late and drunk, to find his house burgled and his wife murdered.

He took the machine with him as well, and dropped it, along with the knife in to the river.

Fuck the deposit.

# The Meal

## Julia Lufford

"Hey!" cried Helen. "Where are you taking me? This isn't the way to Luigi's."

Instead of taking the road into the town centre, Tom Vaughn had taken a left, and was driving out of Aberystwyth.

"That's right."

"Then where are we going?" she said.

"It's a surprise."

"I thought you were taking me for a romantic meal."

Tom grinned. "Did I say that?"

"Yes, you did." Helen pouted. "I had my hair done especially."

"And very nice it looks, too." Tom glanced at her; she was wearing a floral patterned summer-dress. "That's a new dress, isn't it?"

"Yes, I got it from—"

"Sexy dress for a sexy lady," Tom interrupted, not interested in hearing details of Helen's latest shopping trip.

"Smooth talking devil!"

"I'm a very lucky man," he said, and meant it.

"Just you remember it. Mind you, you're not too bad for an old fellah."

"Less of the old. I'm only just forty-five."

She laughed. "Seven years older than me, darling."

"Planning on trading me in for a younger model, are you?"

"Well that would depend on whether the younger model took me out for a romantic meal when he said he was going to." She smiled happily. Tom might be putting on a bit of weight, and have a hint of grey in his hair, but it wasn't all about looks. He was kind, considerate and fun. He made her feel good about herself and after one disastrous marriage that had been what she needed.

"Very sexy lady," Tom murmured.

Soon they were out of the built up area, and once on the open road, Tom put his foot down.

Helen tried again. "So, where are we going?"

"For a romantic meal, of course."

"Out here?" Helen was sceptical. "A country pub?"

Tom turned off the main road, onto a narrower country road. "Wait and see," he said.

A few miles further on, trees bordered one side of the road, replacing the fields full of sheep. Soon a lane forked from the road, leading into the wood. Tom drove down the lane, shortly reaching a clearing.

"We're here," he announced, stopping the car.

"Where exactly is *here*?" Helen frowned.

"Well, almost, we have to go the rest of the way on foot."

Tom got out of the car, and took a deep breath. "Ah, smell that fresh clean air."

"Never mind the clean air, is it clean underfoot?"

"Come on," Tom urged, opening her door.

Helen got out. "I better not make a mess of my shoes."

"They'll be fine. See that path over there?" He pointed.

She nodded, still sceptical.

"Well, it leads to this wonderful glade."

"Tom, don't tell me your idea of a romantic meal, is eating something you've learned about from a Ray Mears television programme!"

He laughed, opening the boot of the BMW, from which he produced a rug and a large hamper. "Come on then."

"A picnic!" gasped Helen.

"Of course. Close her up, would you? What could be better on a beautiful summer day like today? Why be stuck in Luigi's restaurant?"

"Why indeed?"

"Especially when I had Luigi prepare our picnic."

"Darling, you are wonderful."

"Hurry up then, I'm starving."

The path ended and they stepped into the glade.

"It's beautiful," Helen declared.

Tom set down the picnic basket, and spread out the rug.

"Darling, you are wonderful." She said again, this time embracing him.

"Yes, I am." He pulled her down onto the rug, and they kissed.

"I thought you said you were hungry."

"I have many appetites," he said, grinning. "Now, how about some champagne?"

Tom popped the cork from the bottle and poured drinks for them both.

Tom raised his glass. "To us."

"To us," she echoed. "Umm, that's good."

"Wait until you taste the rest." Tom began unpacking the food. "I've got all your favourites."

They ate in contented silence. And when they'd finished eating Helen declared, "That was delicious."

"Nowhere near as delicious as you." Tom poured more champagne.

"Flattery will get you everywhere!"

"That's what I was hoping." Tom leaned back against a tree.

"Why don't you take that dress off?"

"You what?"

"On such a glorious day, don't you fancy being skyclad?" Tom smiled.

"I never had you down as a hippie, Tom Vaughn."

"Nothing wrong in being at one with nature. Besides…" He left the sentence unfinished.

"Besides, what?"

"You said you'd never done it outside. Well, here's the perfect opportunity."

Helen giggled, "What if someone comes along?"

"Well that just adds an extra frisson of excitement, doesn't it? Come on, no one's going to disturb us. Haven't you noticed how quiet it is?"

She sighed. "Yes, it is peaceful here."

"Go on," Tom urged. "Strip for me."

Helen finished her champagne and stood up. She pulled the straps of her dress from her shoulders, wiggled about in what she hoped was a sexy manner and allowed her dress to fall to the ground.

"Beautiful." Tom stood up. "Here, let me," he said, moving behind her. He undid her bra and his hands cupped her breasts. He kissed the back of her neck.

He released her, allowing her to turn around. "Should have kept some of that whipped cream."

"What?"

"Then I could have licked it off these magnificent tits."

"Tom, what's got into you?"

"I want to get into you," he growled.

They kissed, and she eagerly began to unbutton his shirt.

"No." Tom stopped her. "Really let yourself go!"

Helen's eyes grew large, and Tom nodded.

In response, she took hold of Tom's shirt, and ripped it open; buttons went flying.

"Now that's more like it."

Their lips met again, tongues probing, hands roaming freely over each other's body. Helen reached to undo Tom's trousers, could feel his erection through them.

"No, not yet." Tom stopped her again.

"What?"

"Let's try something different."

"I thought doing it outside *was* something different. So, what have you got in mind, now?"

"Well, as we've decided to try out new things, how about a bit of bondage?"

"Kinky bastard! Seems to me, you've done the deciding."

"Come on, Helen, it'll be fun. Nothing serious, I'll just tie you to that tree. You can tie me up next time."

"Promise?"

"Promise."

"Well hurry up then," Helen urged. "I want you."

*The Meal*

Tom quickly retrieved a rope from the car.

"Now, my woodland nymph, up against this tree."

Helen stood with her back to a tree, and Tom tied her hands behind its trunk. "There, not too tight."

"Ravish me, master," Helen begged.

Tom knelt before Helen, pulled her panties down, and began to kiss her stomach, working his way lower.

Helen began to moan. "Oh Tom, eat me, eat me, oh yeah, oh ye…" Abruptly Helen's cries of pleasure changed to a groan of distress. "Oh nooooo!"

"Helen?" Tom mumbled.

"Tom, stop it, please," she whispered.

"What? What's the matter?" Tom asked. "I thought you were—"

Helen cut him off. "Tom, there's someone coming,"

Tom's face assumed an expression of mock indignation. "Are you accusing me of premature ejaculation?"

"I mean there's someone else in the woods."

"So? That just adds to the fun."

"Tom!"

"Where are they?" he asked.

"Obviously I can't point, but over there." Helen indicated with her head.

"I can't see anyone."

"Tom, you'd better untie me."

"Don't you want them to join in then, lover?" Tom asked. "I suppose it depends what they look like?"

"For God's sake be quiet! They'll hear us."

Tom stared at the far side of the clearing. "I can't see anyone. It's just a tree swaying in the breeze."

"What breeze? There is no breeze. And if there was, why would only one tree be moving? Now, will you untie me? Please."

"Helen, my love, there's nobody there; we are quite alone."

"Oh my God!" Helen gasped.

Into the clearing, a darkness spread. First a shadow, and then the impossible darkness that created that shadow. No tree this, and yet there were similarities.

Orifices covered its pulsating trunk. Orifices that writhed, opening and closing, like mouths, seeping slimy secretions. Orifices within darkness that opened revealing a stygian darkness, blacker than any black they had ever seen before.

And on top, what had appeared to be branches moved questing and grasping, tentacle like appendages, rubbery and obscene.

"Fucking hell!" Tom swore.

Tom had been taken by surprise, but he was a man of limited imagination, and he soon regained his composure. "Don't be ridiculous. There are no such things as monsters."

"Then what the fuck is that!?"

"It's someone dressed up, obviously. They're probably making a film or something."

"But, they do that sort of thing with computers now, don't they?"

"I've got it; they must be filming Doctor Who."

"Doctor Who?" Helen was incredulous. "I don't think they make that rubbish anymore do they?"

"Helen, the Beeb are making it again, doing it all here in Wales, too."

"Tom, the BBC wouldn't come north of the Beacons, even if they were. Good grief! I can't believe we're even discussing this."

Tom remained convinced that his interpretation was correct. "How about it? How do you fancy shagging a monster?" he asked.

The creature stopped, as if sniffing the air, then began to shamble around the clearing, its strange appendages probing the air.

"For God's sake Tom, have you gone mad? Shut up, and untie me."

"I'll take it that's a no then." Tom sounded disappointed.

Helen gave a cry, "Oh shit, it's seen us." She began to

struggle, trying to free herself.

Tom took a step towards the monster, "Hey clear off pervert! This is a private party."

As he got closer Tom realised that this hideous monstrosity out of some horror film was something that was most definitely alive and real, however unbelievable. It was something that killed Tom's sexual fantasies. For a moment he was paralysed, his only movement the tremors that racked his body. And then he ran, terrified like never before

"Tom, where are you going? Don't leave me, Tom. No please... Tom!" Helen screamed her last coherent words.

A flailing appendage caressed Helen's face; another that ended in a sucker clamped over a nipple. The creature contemplated the woman that struggled to free herself and screamed and screamed. It felt good, this being's suffering. It knew there was another of these human beings present; the thing of darkness pursued it. The female of the species was going nowhere.

Tom tried to control his breathing, tried not to move a muscle or make a sound, silently he prayed: *Please God let me get out of here alive.* The monster was shuffling around; he could hear it getting closer. The creature paused; it was near by; sniffing the air trying to smell his scent; the smell of fear. It turned so that it was looking directly at the bushes that Tom was hiding behind, surely it must see him. Abruptly it turned again and moved away. He couldn't believe his luck; the monster had somehow missed him. He thanked God. He should be able to escape; he would escape. He had no thought of rescuing Helen; in fact he had forgotten her. Just a moment more and he could make a dash to his car.

It was quiet apart from the noise made by the creature as it moved away from where Tom was hiding.

The silence was abruptly broken by the James Bond theme; the ring tone of his mobile phone. Before Tom could silence it, the monster had heard it and knew where he was.

The creature moved with surprising speed. It had him in its

grip. Tom screamed.

Still ringing, the phone fell to the ground. Upon impact the answer button was knocked and he heard a familiar voice say: "Hello, darling. I was just ringing to see if you're all right? What time you'd be home? And what would you like for your tea?" It was Barbara Vaughn, his devoted wife.

Tom screamed again as cavernous jaws gaped above him

# ONION

## L. H. Maynard & M. P. N. Sims

As a rule, in my recent experience, Thursdays are quiet. That night though, for some reason, there were groups of people in clumps, like barriers between the drinks and me. The pub was crowded, and noisy, and getting served was an ordeal. It was as if I had to break down walls of physical resistance just to be able to lean on the damp bar. Luckily I'd eaten at home, a microwaved meal for one but at least it was hot, so I didn't have to wait for food to be cooked. I just needed a couple of pints to guarantee sleep.

Some evenings pass quickly and some pass slowly. It isn't always an indicator of enjoyment or lack of it. Some evenings pass slowly because they seem to exist within their own time dimension, as if time has slowed to allow a full appreciation of events. Normally weeks can pass by with life merging into a massive blur of ordinary daily routines. Then, without warning, an average day becomes different and changes the axis of experience. I suppose sometimes that can lead to good things happening as well.

The first time I saw her was during one of those evenings. Those evenings that occur every now and again, when time does seem to move more slowly, and experiences, however normal, take on different aspects.

A lot of people were smoking in the pub and there were layers of haze in the air, almost, but not quite, obscuring the people in the adjoining bar. She was standing holding a clear drink when I saw her. I probably held her glance a second or so too long but if I did it was involuntary, a result of the poor vision in the place rather than a signal of interest. The last thing I wanted was another relationship.

I paid for my pint of bitter. Terry, the landlord, gave me a shrug of resignation that was designed as an apology for the intrusion into my regular peaceful routine. He was used, as I was, to Thursdays being a peaceful evening. A few regulars, crosswords in newspapers, conversations about television programmes, just quiet drinks in quiet lives.

It hadn't always been like that for me. There was a time, quite recently, when life had been hectic, and anything but quiet. That was before Melinda left me. We were married for eleven years so I suppose I had begun to think it was forever. Okay there were no children and that apparently became an issue with her. She never mentioned it to me though, not until it was too late.

We were the perfect couple, everyone always told us that. So well suited that there was genuine shock when we split. Resentment as well, as if the end of our marriage somehow threatened the relationships of our friends. How many of those friends were supportive, and how many drifted away still surprises me even now.

It was shortly after she moved out that the regular visits to the pub became part of my routine. When she moved in with Don, the visits, and the drinks, became even more regular.

As I fought my way to the bar for my second pint that night, I glanced over into the other bar. She was looking directly at me. The woman I'd noticed before. She was with someone; he had his back to me but he looked as if he was quite animatedly trying to make a point to impress her. She didn't look impressed, in fact she looked as if she wanted to leave. She smiled at me and pushed back a fold of fair hair.

She was about my age I guessed, which made her late thirties. I say her hair was fair, but it had lots of highlights, which winced in the artificial lighting. She was attractive, which is why I looked at her in the first place, although her mouth was a little too wide, as if it was straining to say more than she would allow it.

I smiled back at her and raised my glass in a half salute. Her smile widened further, and her companion obviously thought it was in appreciation of whatever he was saying, judging by his body language.

The truth was, I realised as I sat back at my solitary table by the fire, that I was still in a kind of shock from Melinda leaving me. Not just ending the marriage but conducting an affair for months before she told me. Any decent relationship is built on trust and honesty. With that wrecked by Melinda's actions my mind was constantly remembering things she had said and done, milestones we had shared, and doubting if any of it ever meant anything to her.

The second pint was almost finished, and I knew I was on course for at least a couple more. I recognised the maudlin mood my memories were making. I began to stand, glass in hand, when I collided with someone. I turned to apologise, as we British always do even when it's not our fault, and looked into the wide smile of the woman from the other bar.

She took a step backwards, glanced up and her smile became more amused when she saw who she'd bumped into. "Must be fate," she said. Her voice was soft with a hint of a local accent.

I extricated my legs from my chair in order to fully stand away from the table.

"I'm Jill." She held out her right hand.

My right hand still grasped the now empty pint glass. I quickly put it down, wiped my hands on my top, and took hers. As I touched her hand I felt a jolt through my body. It wasn't a feeling I was familiar with and I could see by the way her dark eyes sparkled that she was aware of my reaction.

"You'd better let go of my hand," she said. "I don't know him well but I would guess my companion is the jealous type."

I snatched back my hand as if she had bitten it. "Sorry. Don't want to upset your boyfriend."

She laughed, and lots of tiny wrinkles around her eyes and mouth widened as if her skin was opening to let something out. "He's not my boyfriend. I only met him tonight. Blind date. Good natured but misguided friends trying to help me find Mr Right."

I grimaced in sympathy. "I know those sort of friends. Well

157

meaning but…"

"Irritating?"

I nodded. "Even so I'd better let you get on with whatever…"

"A tactical visit to the Ladies." She patted her small clutch bag. "Mobile phone call to a more realistic friend to come and rescue me. Not so sure I want rescuing totally though, now I've met you."

My weight shifted from one leg to the other. "You're direct anyway."

"Get your drink, I'll have a red wine, the Merlot, and give me five minutes." With that she manoeuvred her way through to the toilets and was gone.

That was my introduction to Jill.

Close inspection showed me her hair was a fair colour but masked by so many different highlights and tints that I would have had to peel back the layers to find her natural colour. Her skin was pale, subtly enhanced by makeup, and her mouth and eyes ready to smile in an instant.

I got my drink, and the red wine. The journey to the bar was easier this time; the pub was thinning out a bit as it got nearer to closing time. Just as I sat back at the table a man leaned over and spoke into my face. Not aggressive but insistent.

"She won't want just the one," he said, indicating the wine glass. "You're welcome to her." He pushed at the table, making it move without any danger of tipping it over. More a gesture than an act of true violence.

Seconds later Jill sat down opposite me. She had the look of a naughty schoolgirl.

"What did you say to him?" I asked.

"Told him something better had turned up. Thanks for the drink."

I didn't know whether to be pleased to be described as 'something better' or heed the warning bells going off in the rational side of my brain that if she could treat him so casually then perhaps it would soon be my turn. Trouble was that after three pints of beer and seven months of loneliness I wasn't feeling very rational.

We talked for a while. I learned she was a commercial artist, working from home. Home was local, in the next village to mine. She didn't offer the information but I learned she liked a drink, judging by the glasses of wine she consumed. They didn't seem to have any effect on her, not immediately.

And then it was time to leave. Terry called for last orders; a final flurry of alcohol and it was time to make our way home.

She snaked her arm through mine as we walked into a crisp clear night.

"I can't drive you home," I said. "Far too much to drink."

She turned to me, held onto the front of my jacket, and pulled me forwards. Her mouth opened in an insistent kiss that sent waves rippling through me. As she pulled away she dabbed at the corners of her mouth as if she had just consumed a satisfying meal.

"That's got that out of the way," she said.

At that moment all the lights went out. In the darkness I thought I heard Jill murmur.

Terry was standing at the door of the pub. "Sorry about that. I turned the wrong switch, killed all the lights in the whole place, inside and out. Normal service now resumed."

Jill squeezed my hand. "Did that scare you?" She sounded pleased. "Just the landlord turning off a light too many."

But it hadn't been just the pub lights that went out. Every car headlight, every street light, every light in the nearby houses had darkened for a few seconds. It had even seemed as if the moon went into hiding.

A car pulled into the forecourt. It sounded its horn and a woman stuck her head out of the open window. "You were right, Jill. He's gorgeous."

Jill turned to me and hugged me. "My lift home. I rang her from the Ladies." She pressed a piece of paper into my hand. "My email address. We'll meet tomorrow."

With that she ran to the waiting car and sped off into the

night.

It seemed suddenly empty without her, but at least the lights didn't go out again.

The walk home was over in an instant. I was ridiculously excited. I felt in my pocket for the scrap of paper she had given me. Earlier I had told myself I would play it cool and leave any communication until the next day. Now I was home that resolve had gone. The still deadness in the dusty rooms, the slow ticking of the clocks, the absolute silence throughout the cottage, took my determination to wait and crumpled it like a leaf. The only problem was the piece of paper had gone.

I must have lost it somewhere between the pub and home. I hadn't stopped, I couldn't remember touching my pockets at all. I swore profusely. As high as my excitement had taken me, I was now pressed down low. Suddenly all the latent depression the past few months had been slowly revealing peeled away, and I felt a weight of sadness I had never known before. I cried like a baby.

It seemed to last for hours but could only have been a few minutes. I wiped my eyes on my sleeve and blew my nose on some paper towel from the kitchen. Just off the kitchen is a small room I use as a study. The computer screen was blinking at me. I had an email message.

*Hi lover. Just got in. Didn't stop talking about you on the way home. Ciara is sick of you already! (Joke) Couldn't stop thinking about you so have gone to bed to dream of you doing naughty things to me. Come round tomorrow. My address is attached. It's virus free so you can open it safely. (So am I!! And you can open me as well ;-) ) Love you, J, xxxx*

She loved me. She couldn't possibly. But she did. I went to bed and all I could think of was sex. If the warning bells were sounding again they were so muted I could ignore them with ease. They were drowned in beer and arousal.

In the morning some kind of sanity had been restored. I would go round and see her tonight. We'd have a few drinks, perhaps a takeaway meal. Then, with luck I'd get to sleep with her. No involvement that was what I told myself. No strings, no attachment, no complications. It all sounded so easy.

I found her house at the second attempt. Her village consisted of two pubs, a church, a small row of shops, and curving lanes with houses dotted about at sporadic intervals as if sprinkled like seeds.

Her house was detached, large, and although it was quite a dark evening I could see that some repairs would be needed to allow it to be called smart.

I parked the car in the lane. I was just checking the bunch of flowers I had brought, and the bottle of wine, when the front door of the house opened. A man strode out, anger written in his reddened face and tightly hunched shoulders.

"There's no talking to you when you've had a drink," he shouted.

At the door Jill was holding a wine glass, a genuine smile on her face although the mouth was closed, the lips full and very red. She saw me and waved. The man saw the gesture and glared at me as he approached the end of the drive.

"Who are you?" he demanded.

I shook my head, guessing that whatever I said would be the wrong thing. Anyway I didn't know what I was, not in this context.

The man snorted. He had clearly been drinking. "Oh, don't tell me, the latest pick-up. She's not pissed yet but she will be later, I can see the signs. Seen them before. Give me a call when you're done and I'll pop round for afters."

I knew that even under different circumstances I wouldn't like him, and that knowledge gave me some courage. I hit him. It was an off centre blow but it caught him on the jaw and he went down. I expected him to get up fighting, and I put the flowers and the wine down quickly, just in case. He looked up at me from the gravel path. Then he began crying.

I picked up my things and walked to the front door.

"My hero," Jill said, and hugged me.

I shrugged her off and moved past her into a small entrance

hall. There were black and white drawings on the wall, nudes mostly. I heard the door close and felt her body press against mine. I began to react instinctively although I felt anything but amorous at that moment.

"Who is he?" I asked.

"My husband," she said, and took the bottle of wine and the bunch of flowers from my hands.

The entrance hall became suddenly cold. The stairs ahead of me darkened, and where I could at first see the top of them, now shadows had deepened so that I could barely make out the first step. The ceiling above me felt as if it was compressing downwards, was shrinking towards me, moving to crush me.

Jill grabbed my hand and pulled me into a gold and cream living room. "We're separated," she said, and disappeared into what I guessed was the kitchen.

I sat on a soft sofa and looked around me. The door to the room was open and the shadows still shifted in the hallway.

It was a bright, comfortable room, with books and rugs and pictures. An empty bottle stood on a small wooden table, with two glasses next to it. Her husband, that was unexpected. Separated, to what extent?

Jill re-appeared with fresh glasses and the newly opened bottle of wine.

"Supposed to let it breathe, but you look as if you could do with this."

She left the room and when she came back the flowers were arranged in a delicately cut glass vase.

"I don't remember you mentioning a husband last night."

"Didn't want to spoil the mood. Anyway I told you we're separated. For good, there's no going back. It's been over for years."

She poured two large wines and drank hers back quickly. As she poured herself another I drank a little more slowly.

There was music playing softly in the background, Tim Buckley. Melancholia and regret.

"You know the trouble with you?" she said, as if she had

been considering it for some time.

I sipped my wine and gestured to her to tell me.

"You want to analyse everything too much." She sat back as if she had delivered the meaning of life. Then she leaned forward. "Thinking too much ruins your sex life."

She began unbuttoning her white blouse. I couldn't take my eyes from her full breasts, gradually revealed in a white lace bra. She didn't know me well enough to presume to judge me, but her large nipples edged away from the corners of her clothing and all reason passed away to another place.

Her wide mouth opened in a smile, but I suspect it wasn't of simple satisfaction. It seemed to me, even in my abandonment, to be a smile far more of possession than of mere pleasure.

When we were naked she gave and received with equal measure. What she seemed to like being done to her she liked with noisy approval, and when she gave her attention to me I was transported to an alien land.

At one stage I opened my eyes, her mumbling piquing my curiosity. The walls of the bright room had turned black. There were still spaces where pictures hung on the wall but they were glowing blocks of light. The whole room seemed to be spinning as if we were suspended in space. Yet in the centre of the room I could still see the bottle of wine, with the two empty glasses.

Then she bit down on me and I cried out. She lifted her body from mine and shuffled to the opposite end of the sofa.

"Need a time out?" She smiled. Then I heard a child calling.

A look of anger passed across her face but she masked it swiftly.

I sat up. "Is there a child in the house?" I made a grab for my clothes.

She stood up, sweat glistening on her skin. "It's Peter. My son."

I heard a door open and then shut. She stood and pulled her blouse over her head, it covered her like a very short dress. In the kitchen I could hear shuffling, as if more than one pair of feet were scraping across the floor. Upstairs a door again opened and slammed shut. The corners of the room weren't bright any longer. It was if piles of dust had accumulated for years, and were now moving.

"You'll like Peter," she said happily. "I know he'll love you." She leaned forward and engulfed my mouth in hers. "I know I do."

She left the room and I heard her footsteps running up the stairs. I dressed hastily and carelessly. Don't get involved I had promised myself, and it sounded like good advice.

A few moments went by, and I began to wonder if she wasn't putting the child to bed. I wondered how old he was. Then I realised this was probably the reason the husband had come round. That would be it, access rights. My spirits soared and despite my good intentions I forgot to keep them in check.

I began to glance at the pictures on the walls. Some were prints of classical pieces but some were photographs, mounted to look like pictures. Some were recognisable as fairly recent. Jill in clothes similar to those she wore now. In some she was with a slightly younger version of the angry husband. In some she had a small boy with her; presumably Peter. Some other photos were far older. What looked facially to be Jill, but couldn't be her because the scenes were of fifty years ago at least. The resemblance was so strong that I could only assume it was her mother, or grandmother. The likeness was remarkable.

"And this is Peter."

I turned to see a small blonde boy staring at me as if I was a butterfly on a pin. I guessed his age to be about seven or eight years.

"Hello, Peter," I said, and not knowing quite what to do I held out my hand to him.

He rushed into my arms as if I was a long lost companion.

"Nick!" he cried, and hugged me with an intensity that I found uncomfortable.

Jill helped herself to a glass of wine from a newly opened

bottle. I hadn't seen her open it, or even fetch it from the kitchen.

"That's enough, Peter." She tapped the glass with her fingernail to get his attention. "You'll frighten the poor man away."

Peter pulled away from me and sat on an armchair under the window. "I won't frighten you away will I, Nick?" he said earnestly.

I tried a laugh but it came out more as a groan. "No." I looked at Jill, who was draining her glass. "Your mum will do that."

I smiled at her to indicate I was joking but I could see by the hardening of her eyes that she chose to take the remark seriously. "You think you're so clever, don't you?"

I picked up my own wine glass, but she snatched the bottle and clasped it to her chest. "I was just making a bad joke." I said.

"I don't think you can see me laughing, do you?"

I didn't know what to do, or what to say. I looked towards the window, an involuntary escape route. The curtains were open; hadn't they been drawn? Outside the sunlight danced through the panes, the glare making part of the room brighter than ordinary, and the unlit corners black and bottomless. But it had been evening when I arrived – it should still be evening.

I sat on the sofa. I opened my arms to her. "I'm sorry. I didn't mean to offend you, Jill. I thought we were getting on okay."

She put the bottle down on the table. "Let's have a drink," she said. Her smile was wide again. Open and inviting. Her face was still glowing from our lovemaking, although the wine was applying the second coat.

She poured two large glassfuls. "Peter, do you want a sip?"

Peter crawled on his hands and knees and sat at her feet like a cat. She leaned her glass to his lips and he flicked out his tongue, lapping at the rich liquid. He turned towards me and his look had become challenging.

"Are you going to be my new daddy?"

"Your mummy is very nice." I tried to be as gentle as I could, but my experience with children is limited. "It's very early. We've only just met."

"But you've fucked her, haven't you?"

From the kitchen I heard glass smashing, and crockery, as if items were being pulled from shelves and crashed to the floor.

Jill put down her glass, albeit reluctantly. "Peter, wherever did you hear such language?"

He smiled sweetly at her. "From you, mummy."

She snarled at him. "You most certainly did not." She grabbed him roughly by the arm. "This is your father's doing. It's no coincidence you saw him and now you're using gutter language."

She pulled him from the room and I finished my wine in three long gulps.

When I sat down on the sofa the material seemed to whisper, as if echoes of past occupants were protesting. One of the wine glasses, it must have been Jill's, had tipped over and deep red wine was puddling on the beige carpet.

When Jill came back into the room she was laughing. "Kids," she said. "What would you do with them?"

I thought the way the boy had behaved was abysmal but I thought better of telling Jill that. "Another wine?"

She was kneeling by the table with the stain of wine spreading on the carpet. "Did you do this?"

"Wait a minute…"

She ran into the kitchen, where I could hear her sobbing.

"Jill?"

"Don't come in…"

Yet another opened bottle of wine accompanied her when she came back into the living room. Red-rimmed eyes showed her distress but her mood had swung again. "I haven't seen my mother for six years."

Where did that come from? I was struggling to keep up with her as I realised just how drunk she was. I wanted to get out, and quickly, but I was reluctant to leave her in this state, with her son, however unpleasant he might have been. Out of the corner of my eye I noticed the flowers I had brought. They had withered and died.

"Is this your mother?" I indicated the pictures on the walls.

She shook her head. "You don't understand."

Outside the window it was raining. Night had fallen, or possibly it had always been there.

Jill was unbuttoning her blouse. Her fingers moved surprisingly fluently. She straddled me on the sofa, her large breasts softly insistent on my face. I half-heartedly pushed her away. "Can we talk?"

She gave me a look of disgust. "You've always been intimidated by my nipples haven't you?" She flung herself off the sofa and flounced out of the room. "I'm checking on Peter, don't be here when I come back down."

The room felt overly warm. I couldn't see the corners, they were too dark. The kitchen sounded as if it was full of people whispering, like mourners at a funeral. Some of the pictures on the wall were blank now. Others were cloudy, as if the images were seeping away into the walls behind them.

I felt in my pocket for my car keys. They were there. She had ordered me out and I was more than happy to oblige.

The door to the living room was closed, although I didn't recall Jill shutting it behind her. It was hard to open, as if something was blocking it. It opened inwards but it felt as if someone was pulling against me. Jill? Then it suddenly eased and I opened it, stepping back away from it just in case she was standing there.

The hallway was in complete darkness. I was scared to go into it without any light. I stretched my hand against the wall, feeling for a light switch. The wall felt damp, as if the wallpaper was sweating. My arm reached out, flat against the wall. Then something took hold of my arm and tried to pull me into the darkness.

I recoiled, kicking out in a reflex action. My foot connected with something soft that grunted as I hit it. I kicked out again and I heard it scamper away. It must be a cat, it couldn't be anything else. A dog would have barked. It couldn't be anything else.

Armed with a false burst of courage I jumped into the hall, hammered at the wall and eventually, by chance, my fingers found a switch. A single bulb hanging from the centre of the ceiling flickered into life and I looked around. The entrance hall was the same as I remembered. Except the black and white drawings of the nudes were all obviously Jill, and all depicted her covered in bloodied wounds.

"You're not leaving?"

I heard her voice from the top of the stairs. It sounded calm and seductive. I backed away, closer to the front door.

The top of the stairs was shrouded in shadow, but I could see her begin to move slowly down. She was still naked from the waist up, but the poor light made her body appear to be almost translucent.

My back pressed against the door. I reached up with one arm to locate the lock.

Jill had moved onto an even darker part of the staircase. Her body merged with the darkness, losing its form. It looked as if she had become a shapeless mass, all but flopping down each stair.

The lock needed two hands. In the time it took me to glance away from her to open the door she had moved closer to me. The smile I had thought inviting was now threatening.

I thought her mouth to be a little wide but it was now extending to include her whole face. The lips cracked open, a lolling tongue protruded, and the mouth became so huge the body beneath it seemed to be swallowed inside.

I couldn't see my car outside. It might still be there.

I finally stopped running. Eventually.

## IN SICKNESS AND…

### John Llewellyn Probert

"He's always swearing."

"She's always bloody well complaining about something."

"He's never at home."

"Well one of us has to work for a living! And if I do get home early all I get is an earful of bloody crap. Is it any wonder I have to go to the pub to unwind?"

"If he took me out once in a while maybe I wouldn't be so unhappy."

"If she wasn't so bloody miserable all the time maybe I would take her out."

"He doesn't care about me."

"She's the one who doesn't care. Sitting at home all day. It isn't as if she has to *do* anything other than keep the house tidy."

"That's all I am to you is it? Just a housekeeper? How things have changed."

"You have you mean."

"No you have."

"No *you* have."

"No YOU have."

"I think that's quite enough from the two of you for now, don't you think?"

Marguerite Lucas crossed her legs, leaned back in her swivel chair, and regarded the couple before her with the gaze of someone who considered herself to have over fifteen years' experience in the marriage guidance field. The gold band perched above the diamond-encrusted sapphire engagement ring had enjoyed pride of place on the third finger of her left hand for even longer than that, but she had never felt the urge to flaunt it before those less able to cope with the little difficulties that could be encountered on the sometimes rocky road of marriage as final proof, if proof were needed, that yes

169

she had been married for nearly twenty years, no it hadn't always been easy, but yes if you were determined enough you could make it work. In sickness and in health the vicar had said, and in sickness and in health they had been together and if things hadn't always been perfect then she had made do with almost perfect, just the way her mother had said she should. She was lucky, she supposed, that after all this time she could still leave the house with a goodbye kiss from a loving husband, his 'You take care and have a good day,' still giving her that warm secure feeling it always had.

She turned her attention back to her first client-couple of the day.

Kevin and Jayne Dobson were twenty-four and twenty-three years old respectively and had been married for three years. No children yet but that was the plan eventually. They had married after a romance that had sounded from Jayne's description as less of a whirlwind and more a tepid breeze you probably wouldn't even notice unless you were facing in the right direction. All their friends had been getting married around the same time and it had seemed 'the thing to do'. The post-event depression had been a while in coming but when it did it had kicked in mercilessly, driving Kevin to work longer hours at the office and Jayne to the brink of depression. A visit to the GP later and here they were. They looked as if they were about to start arguing again and so Marguerite cleared her throat to remind them that neither was now allowed to speak until she gave her permission.

"What I want to do," she said, "is talk to the two of you individually. Jayne can go first and have her say in private while Kevin waits outside, and then you can swap round."

Kevin didn't seem too keen.

"This is bollocks," he said. "It's not doing any good at all."

"We'll discuss that at the end," said Marguerite. "As I said to you when you came in, the mere fact that you are here means that you want to save your marriage and that can only be a good thing. A good thing that both of you, deep down, really want."

"And Lorraine is away for how long did you say?" said Jayne.

Marguerite frowned briefly at the name of their usual marriage guidance counsellor.

"As I said when you came in, I'm afraid Lorraine has been unexpectedly called away and so I've been assigned her cases until she's well enough to come back. Now Kevin, you go out to the waiting room. Have you brought something to read?"

Kevin took the latest copy of one of the middle-shelf men's magazines from the plastic bag at his feet.

"Christ I wish he wouldn't read that stuff either," said Jayne.

"And what did you bring to look at?" Marguerite asked her.

Jayne took out her copy of *Modern Chat* which this week boasted several scandalous stories regarding the sexual shenanigans of the slightly rich and vaguely famous.

"Bloody crap," said Kevin.

"Kevin you may leave us now," said Marguerite. "I'll send Jayne out for you when we're finished."

Jayne's husband made an exaggerated display of getting out of the chair, and slammed the door behind him on the way out. As soon as he was gone Marguerite closed their file and pushed it to one side.

"That's a good sign you know," she said.

"What!?" Jayne gave the therapist an incredulous look. She realised she was whispering, even though she had previously been reassured that the door was thick enough that she could shout if she wanted to and Kevin wouldn't hear her.

"Oh yes," said the therapist. "All that aggression means that he loves you. If he was showering you with flowers and chocolates all the time it would just mean that he had something to hide. Now, my methods may seem a little... strange, but here's what I want you to do."

Marguerite leaned forward to become more conspiratorial. Over the next fifteen minutes she gave Jayne her never-fail 'to-do' list, making her write down the salient points so that she didn't forget. By the time Marguerite had finished, Jayne looked quite shocked but Marguerite wasn't bothered – the reaction was almost always the same the first time she gave the girls a good talking to. There was a pause before Jayne said:

"Are you sure?"

Marguerite nodded.

"Absolutely," she said. "Just do what I've told you and you'll start to notice the difference."

"But," said Jayne, studying the scrap of paper in her hand. "This looks like a list of things that'll just make him hate me all the more. Iron burns on his shirts? Not cooking his food properly? Forgetting to pay bills? Losing things like our credit cards? Are you sure all this is going to help?"

Marguerite reached over and squeezed her hand.

"Believe me," she said, "if he stays with you despite you doing all these things then that will prove he must love you, won't it? It's just a test that's all. To prove his fidelity and his love for you. And once we are both satisfied that he loves you more than anything we can move onto the next step." She picked up a blue ballpoint pen and briskly thumbed the button. "Now tell Kevin he can come in, and you go and sit outside and take a quiet moment to think about what I've said while I talk to your husband."

*

"No sex?!" Kevin spluttered.

Marguerite had found that a straightforward approach, one that was serious rather than sympathetic, worked better with the men.

"Don't you see it's just another way she has of controlling you? To get her own way? By denying her you're reasserting your self control, showing her that you don't need her. And if she really loves you she'll stay but she'll know it has to be on your terms."

Kevin scratched his head and put down his magazine.

Marguerite could guess which pages had been thumbed the most.

"I just don't understand how—"

"I am trying," she snapped, "to help you. To save you. Both of you. But of course if you want to carry on ruining each others' lives be my guest."

Jayne was called back in and Marguerite addressed them both.

"Now the two of you know what you have to do. I'll arrange for another appointment next month so that we can see how things are going." By which time Marguerite would be long gone and someone else could explain to them that their boring, hopeless little marriage was over.

Once they had left she grimaced to herself. Those two obviously weren't meant for each other, and she considered it her job – no, her duty – to make them realise that through gentle persuasion. She was a firm believer that each person in this world had a soul mate, a literal 'other half', and that the coming together of those two people produced a oneness of such harmoniousness that the petty arguments that seemed to make up the major part of Kevin and Jayne's life were inconceivable. No, she had decided, those two were not meant for each other, and they needed to realise that as soon as possible, even if it meant her having to force them apart.

There was a knock on the door. She took a moment to ready herself for her next clients of the morning before offering them a cheery, "Come in."

\*

David and Jemma Parkinson were self-proclaimed upper middle class, lived in one of the smarter areas of town, had three lovely children, and hated each other with a passion matched only by Jemma's fondness for gin and tonics and David's for anything on which he could place a bet. Despite the proximity of the local racecourse David was doing his best to keep his gambling under control. From the excess of perfume she wore and the way she was having to concentrate hard on sitting upright, Jemma didn't seem to be doing so well and was receiving separate counselling for her alcoholism. Their home life consisted of David making regular sweeps of the house for hidden gin bottles and trying to improve his wife's self-esteem while popping out from time to time to gamblers anonymous meetings. Jemma, on the other hand, possessed the unshakeable belief that her husband kept leaving the house to conduct one of the numerous affairs she was convinced he was having, possibly including one with her own sister. Her days consisted of fruitlessly trying to prove this while at the same time constantly rotating the hiding places of her stash of alcohol. Remarkably they had somehow managed to avoid involving the children in all of this.

But it would only be a matter of time, Marguerite thought, as she offered them the kind of advice that would be sure to get David into even more trouble and guarantee Jemma a breakdown. But at least then the children would have the benefit of a fresh start.

Her third, and final, couple of the morning, was an entirely different affair. Certainly there had been a few little misunderstandings, mostly due to some insecurity on both their parts, but the way they looked at each other, sat as close together as they could, and the way they kept touching each other for reassurance made Marguerite think of how things had once been for her. Of course not everything was quite right for them but she gave them the best advice she could think of before wishing them well as they left.

It was lovely to finish her morning on an upbeat note, she thought, as she tidied her notes away. Those two were almost perfect for each other and sometimes you had to make the odd concession. Sometimes you had to make do with almost. They, too, had asked where Lorraine was. Of course the most amusing thing was that Lorraine hadn't gone anywhere. In fact during all of this morning's consultations she hadn't even left the office. Of course she wasn't in the sort of condition to be able to listen to any of her former clients' problems, not with most of her in the metal cupboard behind the desk and the bits that Marguerite couldn't quite fit in sawn off and secreted in the desk drawer, the box files on the shelf in the corner (thank goodness they were red!) and beneath the leaves of the banana plant by the door, covered by a thin layer of earth that was doing an excellent job of stopping the smell from becoming too obvious. Sometimes her carefully arranged plans did go awry but she liked to think she could take care of any eventuality, and so when the meddling woman had come into work anyway despite Marguerite's letter 'from the council' (on official paper that she had stolen, too!) saying that reports of a gas leak had meant that no-one would be allowed into the building until it had been checked out, Marguerite had had to think quickly.

"You don't look like someone from the gas board," Lorraine had sniffed as she had interrupted Marguerite's preparations for the morning. "And I can't smell gas."

The smell, Marguerite had explained, appeared to be emanating from the radiator that was conveniently positioned furthest from the window. As the younger and stronger-looking woman had bent over to inspect the area Marguerite had quickly slipped the flex from the desk lamp around her throat and held on for dear life as the bloody woman had done her best to throw herself around the room. Eventually, her face as purple as the hideous varnish on her fingernails, Lorraine Marsden had collapsed, dead, to the floor.

Just as Kevin and Jayne had knocked on the door.

"I'll be with you in a minute!" Marguerite had cried, while at the same time realising that their counsellor wouldn't fit in the big metal cabinet behind the desk. There had been nowhere else to hide the body and so, priding herself on her resourcefulness, she had taken her nail scissors from her handbag and... trimmed Lorraine to fit, disposing of the excess around the office. Finally, with the cupboard door wedged shut and the red stickiness on her fingers removed with a moistened towelette she had been ready to start work for the day.

\*

Marguerite Lucas wasn't her real name, and as she waited for the train to take her back to her home nearly sixty miles away the woman who had been the subject of a number of tabloid headlines many years ago for what had been deemed 'atrocities', began to think about who she could pretend to be the next time she decided to give herself a little treat. After all, she had been pronounced cured by those lovely people at the hospital, and she believed the papers had even written headlines about how wonderful it was that she could be allowed back into the community when she had been released. She loved working with people but so rarely got the chance to do so. In fact after almost getting into more trouble with the authorities a couple of years ago she now limited her counselling sessions to once a year, taking care to find somewhere far away from where she and her husband lived to minimise any potential fuss.

Before she knew it she was back in her home town, walking through leafy suburbs until she came to the modern two-bedroomed house on the estate where she lived. She checked herself one last time for any telltale bloodstains and then slid the key into the lock.

"I'm home!" she cried.

"Hello darling – I'm in the lounge," came the reply.

She popped upstairs to hang up her jacket and change out of her work shirt into something a bit more suited to being at home

Her husband Roger was sitting by the window in his favourite armchair, an open book on his lap. It was a dull day and so he had the lamp on to read by, the curtains drawn closed to avoid the attention of passers-by. He had always hated people looking in through the window.

She brushed his dry cheek with her lips and asked him how his day had been.

"Oh, the same, you know?" was the reply. "How was yours?"

"Fine," said Marguerite with a smile. "Now how about a hug for your wife?"

The top she had changed into had a set of hooks sewn into the back so that when she manoeuvred his arms around her the metal rings she had screwed into the bone of each of his fingertips caught and held so that his embrace didn't slip, allowing her to hug him as well. There was the slightest crunching sound as she squeezed him, reminding her that she needed to be a little gentler than she would ideally like. She felt herself relaxing in his arms, the worries of the day leaving her just like they always did.

Once she felt more like her old self she gave a little jerk downwards to unhook his fingertips, catching his arms as they fell and replacing them so that his hands were folded in his lap.

"What would you like for tea?" she asked.

"Oh, I've already eaten," said his voice from the speaker hidden behind the antimacassar. "You get yourself something, though."

"All right," she said, turning to the stereo system by the door and pondering whether or not she should change the compact disk that was currently playing.

There were a number of ways to activate the dialogue tracks and get her husband to say what she wanted to hear. The remote control she was currently holding was one, then there were the various pressure pads in the kitchen, the bathroom, and of course the bedroom. Opening the front door automatically triggered the first track of whichever disk she had inserted before leaving the house that morning so that one of the greeting messages would play when she came home.

She looked around the lounge. So little space, she thought. In fact there was hardly room for Roger and his chair. The rest of the room was filled from floor to ceiling with shelves crammed with silver disks. Thanks to modern computer technology she had finally been able to dump the magnetic tape reels she had used for the original analogue recordings but the conversion to digital format hadn't freed up as much space as she had hoped.

She looked at the rows upon rows of recordings in front of her, remembering how difficult it had been to get him to say all those words, all those sentences, and in some cases all those long paragraphs, just the way she wanted. Of course she had appreciated that it had been difficult for him. In fact he hadn't even wanted to do it at first. It had only been when she had threatened to puncture his throat with the blade she was holding against it, the microphone held against his mouth with the other hand, that he had finally realised how much she loved him and why she needed him to do it.

She smiled to herself. She had got him to talk more in those last two weeks of his life than in their entire two years of marriage. Even at the very end, when he had become too sick to move, she had been able to get him to utter the last few phrases she needed to keep him with her for always.

She winced a little at the memory of when she had first thought things were going wrong between them. Despite his protestations she had been convinced that his impotence was because he was tiring of her. How could she have known it was the first sign of the spinal cancer that had so quickly rendered him paralysed from the waist down?

By the time she had realised that the weakness in his legs wasn't the result of the secret drinking he had always denied they had barely spoken for a month, and being a typical man he had done his best to ignore his symptoms until things were too far gone for anyone to be able to do anything about it. Every now and then, if she wasn't careful, she still found herself resenting him for that.

As they had left the specialist's clinic that day, having been shown scans of Roger's bones littered with lumpy deposits that had no right to be there, the doctor's voice had played over and over in her head. Her husband was going to die. After only being married for two years Roger was going away, making her a widow, leaving her alone in this unfriendly world.

That night she had lain in bed doing her best to ignore her husband's shallow breathing and the intermittent jerks of his legs – movements over which he had little control. In fact it was those involuntary twitches that had first sown the seeds of her plan, and by the time the early morning sunshine was slicing through the gaps in the curtains she had worked out what she wanted to do. It had involved a lot of research, a lot of study, and an awful lot of hard work. But in the end it had been worth it.

Now he would never leave her.

In sickness and in health the vicar had said. Well, in sickness and in death was good enough for Marguerite. After all, almost all the letters were the same.

And sometimes you had to make do with almost.

# THE PIT

## Rog Pile

It was last summer that my sister Marion and her husband Thomas were killed in a car wreck. It was one of those shockingly sudden, out of the blue things, mercifully quick. A lorry carrying a heavy load of steel girders shed its load as it came around a wide bend. One of the girders shot straight through the windscreen of their car and sheared off the roof. Marion had been in the front with Tom, and there hadn't been much left of either of them.

The boy, James, was a lanky, tow-headed creature, rather tall for his ten years. He had no recollection of the accident. He came out of it without a scratch, and all anyone could guess was that he had been lying asleep on the back seat. At this point my other sister, Martha, promptly decided that an orphanage was no place for any child with 'our blood' in its veins, and decided that James should come to live with us.

'Us', I should explain, meant Martha, her husband Alex, their son Edward, and me. There was never any fear that we would be overcrowded. The house which we shared was easily large enough to house our little family twice over. The irony that the house had been left to me by my father, the only one of his three children who had never married nor shown even the least inclination to start a family, was a constant thorn in Martha's side. It was just her bad luck, I suppose, that father had been rather old fashioned and had preferred to leave the bulk of his estate to his son.

I had the west wing entirely to myself, and when Alex was away on business, several days often went by without my needing to venture into the other half of the house and encounter the others – which suited me, because I have always preferred my own company.

The atmosphere was strained the day that James arrived. Edward had been elusive most of the day, probably knowing that I wanted to talk to him about the imminent arrival; I guessed that he was feeling pretty confused. He was a sensitive sort of boy, who sometimes needed reassuring. I was working at my desk, which is in a corner window overlooking the drive and a broad sweep of the gardens, when I saw the taxi crawl up the drive like a gleaming black beetle. It stopped at the front door and doors opened on either side, like beetle wings, and I saw James climb out, stiff and uncomfortable in Sunday black, pale hair licking down over his eyes. The driver walked around the car and began dragging suitcases from the boot and carrying them inside, while Martha hugged James (obviously stiff and unresponsive, even from this distance, though I couldn't blame him, caught in Martha's grip); then she tipped the driver and led the way into the house. After another moment I noticed a small figure moving furtively across the drive. It was Edward; he must have been there the whole time, perhaps hiding behind the screen of laurel bushes. I watched him until he vanished inside

Half an hour later there was a sharp rap on my door and Martha entered. "We're going to have trouble with those two," she said.

I almost had to admire the casual way that she roped me in to share the responsibility. It was Martha's idea to have James live here, and he was to live in Martha's half of the house; but now *we* were going to have trouble. She glanced around disapprovingly at the bookshelves and the scattering of papers on the floor; her hands twisting the ends of her apron strings in the way she had when some plan was not running as smoothly as it ought. I knew what was coming next, but I decided not to go down without a fight.

"They're quarrelling?"

"No, not that. They just seem, well, *quiet*. It seems unnatural. I keep thinking they're just waiting till my back's turned, then they're going to do some horrible mischief to one another."

"You can't expect not to have some trouble with them.

They're not used to other kids; neither of them has had to share their parents' attention before."

"It's a pity you never married. If you had, we'd never have this problem now. James could live with you. It's unnatural, that's what I call it, living here in this massive house all alone." She sniffed and ran the back of her hand quickly across her nose.

Useless to point out that if I had married, I would possibly have had a child of my own; useless to remind her that I only used half of the house. But I was used to this little speech by now and just let it roll over me. When she seemed to run out of steam, I said, "It's a matter of territory. Edward's grown up here, he's established this place as his home. He resents a stranger coming in, taking over what he sees as his. James feels awkward; there's nothing familiar left to him, even his parents have gone. He's got to come to terms with that."

Martha was giving me an 'I'm not an idiot, get to the point' look.

"You'll have to put them on some sort of neutral ground, some place where neither of them has any sort of advantage and they can have time to get used to one another."

"You mean like the seaside."

"The seaside would be fine. Why don't you get Alex to take you all down the next time he's home?"

"That's one of the things I've been meaning to talk to you about. You know Alex is terribly busy right now, I hardly see him from one week to the next." And within the next few minutes she had persuaded me that it was positively unhealthy the way that I never got any sun or fresh air, and my car would be all the better for a good run, it was bad for the tyres after all to just let it stand, and inevitably it was arranged that I should run them all down to the seaside on the first warm day we had.

The beach brings out the worst in me. I hate having to find a clear spot in the sand, away from all those hundreds of nearly naked bodies. The sun dazzles off the pages of the book you're reading and makes your eyes ache. Sand grits against your teeth when you eat or drink. You try to write and the paper keeps blowing away.

Only Martha seemed really content. She lay back in her hired deck-chair, with her skirt rolled up over her plump knees, eyes closed behind her sunglasses, only awakening now and again to read another chapter from the thick romantic novel spread open across her lap.

At first it looked like they wouldn't get on; my clever scheme to ease them into friendship was seemingly doomed to failure. Crawling about, digging holes in the sand, they watched one another with suspicion, only just barely polite in deference to Martha and me looking on. It was obvious that they were only waiting for a moment when our adult gaze should stray and some petty excuse present itself, to launch an unrestrained attack on one another.

But oddly, it never happened. It was like waiting for a sneeze; you know, when your nose tickles, but the sneeze won't come? Only in this case it didn't come at all. The explosion of childish rivalry that we were all waiting for, handkerchiefs at the ready never happened; instead, the boys' mutual suspicion was replaced by a closeness verging on secrecy.

Several times over the next few days the two of them wandered off together, vanishing for hours at a time. When they came back I never heard them discuss where they had been, they rarely exchanged more than a monosyllable in our hearing. And once, when I tentatively asked Edward if he'd had a pleasant walk, he pretended not to hear; and at that moment, as if on a prearranged signal, James jumped to his feet and threw some sand at us and the two of them immediately rushed away laughing across the beach.

Somehow I found this curious intimacy far more disturbing than any overt act of violence could have been. Perhaps I felt a little left out, too, snubbed even; I had always liked to think of myself as Edward's confidant. Martha, of course, was delighted by the turn of events. But I was becoming more and more curious about how they spent those long afternoon walks, and at the same time I realised I was actually becoming uncomfortable in their presence, as if I was somehow intruding where I was not welcome.

One afternoon there was a very low tide. I'd never seen the water retreat so far, and despite my feelings about the beach, it fascinated me. Martha, as usual, had fallen asleep in her chair, and I was restless from too much inactivity and decided to go for a walk. The shoreline was very much changed. Out in the distance, where we had occasionally seen motor cruisers plying to and fro, people were standing barely up to their waists in placid water.

Previously the sea had made it impossible to walk around the buttress of cliffs, but now it had withdrawn so far that I was able to walk completely around onto a damp, rocky expanse which I supposed was normally occupied only by seabirds or the occasional determined climber.

At first I thought that the beach was deserted, but then I saw the two boys in the distance. I recognised them from the colour of their swimming trunks and James's hair. James in red and Edward in black; James's head of distinctive blonde hair gleaming in the sun. They had climbed to the top of a ridge and stood outlined briefly against the sky. Then they disappeared down the other side.

It was easy to lose all sense of distance and time out here. I began to make my way along the beach, which was really just ridge after ridge of black rock stretching from the cliffs to the sea, pockmarked with small deep pools in whose clear depths brilliant coloured weeds moved. Long beds of sand stretched between the ridges, pitted where the boys had jumped down and landed hard on their heels. I slipped about on the black rocks, following in their tracks. It's a funny thing about those spines of rock, the way they never seem to dry out even if the tide is out for hours. Once, I put my foot in a rock pool; the water was so clear I didn't even see it. By the time I reached the ridge where I'd seen the boys, I was in an irritable mood; I wished I'd brought my cigarettes. The sounds of the holidaymakers behind me had died away completely now, and it was as if I'd entered another country, a secret place.

The boys were nowhere in sight, but they had left a trail. Directly below in one of those long troughs of sand, clearly imprinted in it, were their footprints. I climbed down. The prints led out to the centre of the trough, then turned sharply in towards the cliff. A dark shadow on the cliff face resolved itself into a cave mouth. I noticed some other marks in the sand, which puzzled me. A deep furrow, as if some heavy weight had been dragged, with curious scuff marks either side of it. Clearly the boys had seen these marks, too, and followed them back to the cliff.

The trail disappeared inside the cave. The arched roof was nearly level with my head, but when I made my way in a few yards, it opened up. Boulders jutted out of the sandy floor, indistinct in the half-light from the entrance, but giving some idea of the cave's size. In places, the rock receded into blackness, where other tunnels led away. I guessed the boys were exploring one of these. I heard a muffled giggle and called out, but there was no answer, and I decided they must be playing some game.

I was startled by a shuffling sound close by. My eyes were adjusting to the dark, and I could just make out the long shape lying near the rock wall. For an awful moment I thought that it was a dead body; and in a way, I wasn't far wrong. By the light of a match I saw the blotchy shape of a seal. It was so still that I wondered if it was dead, then it moved suddenly and produced the shuffling noise again with its flippers against the sand. At least I'd solved the mystery of the curious tracks. I inspected the seal more closely and saw mucus streaming from its eyes and nostrils. Like most people, I'd forgotten about the epidemic of seal flu, but it was evidently still taking its toll here on these isolated beaches. The animal was having great difficulty breathing, and from its agitated movements and wheezing I guessed that it hadn't long to live. I wondered if I

185

could shorten its suffering by braining it with a rock, but after casting about in the murk for a suitably sized one I gave up, afraid in case I botched the job.

All this time I had the unpleasant sensation of being watched. The boys' footprints led here, and I was certain that right now they were concealed in some niche close by, watching and giggling under their breath. There was something unwholesome about this idea which made my scalp prickle.

The seal coughed and retched up more mucus, and I backed away out of the cave, intending to find someone who could deal with it. Looking back now it seems strange, but at that time I did not feel the least concern for the boys' safety; it didn't cross my mind for an instant that they might be in danger.

Nearly half an hour later I returned, breasting the black ridge of rock with two coastguards, only to look down into a swirling black channel, where dark water lapped and slopped up the rocky sides at us. The mouth of the cave was submerged except for a scant six inches or so, air under pressure bubbling out in a white froth. There was no sign of the boys.

"Maybe it's just as well," one of the men said. "It'd be too weak to swim, from what you said, sir. This'll be a more natural sort of death for it. It'll be gone by now, for sure."

I felt trapped by indecision; it seemed absurd to mention the boys now after I had brought these men here on account of a seal. Then I wondered what sort of man they would think I was if they suspected that I'd put an animal before the safety of two children. I felt a dull kind of horror when I thought of them, but it was horror of a confused sort. I felt a petulant sort of annoyance towards the children for putting me in this embarrassing position. I realised with a distinct jolt that I actually did not care if they were dead. It was as if I had somehow split in two, and one part of me was now standing in judgement of the other. I knew I had broken some sort of moral code, but it was their fault that I had done so.

I walked back to the beach and sat down in the chair beside

Martha, who was reclining with eyes closed, possibly asleep. I closed my own eyes and tried to think. I wondered if anyone else had seen me following the boys along the beach.

"Have a nice walk?" Martha asked, after a moment or two.

"Not bad. I was looking for the boys."

"Here's James now."

I opened my eyes in time to see him plump down in the sand in front of us. He seemed to be smiling, but it could have been the sun in his eyes. Edward appeared and squatted beside him. Martha repeated her question about the nice walk, and they said yes they'd had a good long walk, but they said nothing about the deserted beach or the cave. I was almost prepared to believe that my eyes had played tricks on me, or perhaps I'd seen two other similar small boys disappearing over that ridge of black rock.

For a fortnight after that I diligently scoured all the local papers, looking for any mention of missing children, or drownings of any sort. Eventually I decided that I was building a mystery out of nothing. The boys, if it had been them, had either followed me back from the cave, keeping out of sight, or continued along the beach until they found some other path up the cliff to safety. Probably it was their idea of a joke; no doubt they'd expected me to alert the coastguard to their disappearance. Whatever the truth, there was obviously a guardian angel of grubby, secretive small boys whom they were working to death with their tricks.

I was up in my room, trying to write, when I heard Martha's knock on the door. I groaned inwardly as she came in, giving up all thought of getting any more work done today. She was dressed in her going out clothes, a bright red bandana, a black duster coat, a rust coloured blouse topping a black skirt and sandals. It had probably looked fine on the shop window mannequin. "Alex won't be home till late, and I've just got to get into town. Do you think you could keep an eye on the boys for the afternoon?"

I said that I probably could.

## The Pit

"It'll do you good, anyway, if you just take a walk around the garden instead of sitting up here alone all the time. What are you writing about anyway? No, don't tell me, I really haven't time now." The door closed behind her, gently lifting some papers from my desk with the draught.

Later, I went into the garden. The house was bathed in bright summer sunshine. Before she left, Martha had pulled the curtains against the glare, so that the furniture wouldn't fade, and now I thought that the windows slightly resembled heavily lidded eyes. This kind of imagery doesn't often suggest itself to me; generally I dislike any sort of anthropomorphism. But just lately I seemed to be seeing mysteries in the most banal, everyday things.

The children in particular seemed more and more wrapped up in some conspiracy of their own devising since the trip to the beach, and were spending most of their time out of sight of the house now, in the surrounding woods and fields. I felt divided between a need to keep an eye on them, in case they might be planning another unpleasant trick, and a primitive sort of instinct that insisted I would be better off keeping a good distance.

I tried to shrug off these ideas. Somewhere in the house Martha had left a radio turned on and the music of a classical guitar thrummed through the air. I walked quietly, eyes almost closed, and let the sound fill me. There was one moment when I felt a prickling, tingling sensation moving over my skin, and I seemed to be ascending physically into the air. Such a moment transforms a day, puts all the petty worries into perspective. I was near the foot of the garden now, deep in the trees, where garden growth merged with the woods. Following the narrow path through this untended shrubbery, which had almost reverted to its original wild state, I came upon them sitting beneath a tree in a clearing. They looked up as I approached. I felt confused; I wanted to keep walking straight by them, but I knew I wouldn't be able. I knew what a mouse cornered by a

188

cat must feel like; at the slightest movement, to be pounced upon.

James scraped at the earth near his heel with a twig. "We've been waiting to talk with you, Uncle. I've heard so much about you. Eddie's been telling me all about the times the two of you had together, when Aunt Martha and Alex have been away."

Edward said nothing but sat quietly watching me with large dark eyes that a girl might have envied. I looked from one boy to the other. Edward turned his eyes away when I looked straight at him, but James met my gaze with his own pale blue stare.

"Things have to change, Uncle," he said. "We've decided, and there's nothing you can do about it." In the same tone he added, "We saw you in the cave. We hid when you came in. We guessed you'd be worried in case Edward was telling tales out of school."

Edward spoke at last, "You'd have let us drown; you told no-one!"

I knew I had to say something, but traps seemed to lie in every direction. I remembered the water slopping at the mouth of the cave, thinking no-one could survive in there. If I denied following them into the cave, I'd fool no-one; if I admitted it, it would be an admission of guilt; either way, they'd gained a hold over me.

"If the others, Aunt Martha and Alex, knew about any of this they'd know there was something really wrong with you."

"What do you mean, 'wrong' with me?"

A bored note entered James's voice. "Oh come on, you must know they already think you're pretty weird, living here on your own with no girlfriend or anything. They might not put the law on you, for Eddie's sake, but if they thought you'd left us to drown and not even said anything, they'd want a lot more to keep quiet about it than we'd ask. You know how they resent you getting the house."

"What do you want?" The words came out impulsively and irrevocably.

"Cigarettes," James said without hesitation. "And air gun pellets; they won't sell them to us in the village."

"And nails, long ones, for the scarecrow," put in Edward; then he looked rather shamefacedly at the ground as James glared at him.

"All right," I said, trying to invest my voice with a jocularity that I didn't feel, as if this were some jolly game of 'let's pretend'. "I'll bring the air gun pellets and the nails down to the shed tomorrow. And... we'll see about the cigarettes." It was horribly humiliating, but I didn't seem to have any choice. I wondered, though, what Edward had meant by the 'scarecrow'. It was probably just some childish secret, but it was obviously important to them.

Over the next few weeks I tried to learn where the boys went, when they disappeared into the woods. Their demands hadn't been excessive (they had once demanded a bottle of gin, but Edward had been ill all the next day). All the same, I couldn't get rid of the fear that at any time they might ask some impossible thing. And all the time I was digging a bigger hole, incriminating myself, by conceding to their demands. The only solution was to beat them at their own game. If I could only learn what they got up to in the woods, I might be able to turn the tables on them.

Trailing the boys was more difficult than I'd expected, it wasn't easy following two agile young boys undetected and I had to keep a safe distance. Once, quite deep in the trees, I thought I smelled wood smoke, but I couldn't trace the fire. Several times I wandered about for hours until the silence began to get on my nerves and I wondered if they had spotted me; were even now watching from behind the undergrowth, faces tiger-striped with lipstick war paint stolen from Martha's bedroom.

Then one day I heard the sharp report of an air rifle from the west side of the wood. I made my way quickly through the trees, and finally forced my way through the last tangle of undergrowth, only to come up against a barbed wire fence which bordered a sloping ploughed field. Out in the centre of the field was a scarecrow. I remembered Edward's cryptic remark and waited for a while, out of sight in the bushes; but if they had been around here they did not reappear.

The next day I saw James stealing away from the garden shed with a coil of rope. It was orange nylon rope, and very long. The rope told me a lot; suddenly I was sure that I knew where they disappeared to each afternoon.

This area is honeycombed with old mine shafts and tunnels; it's the same all over the county. Only a few of the shafts are properly capped. The uncapped mines look like bramble-covered burial mounds to the uneducated eye, and they are usually surrounded by a bit of loose fencing, enough to deter the occasional cow, but an open invitation to adventurous small boys. Some of the shafts only go down ten or twenty feet.

Next day I followed them through the woods again. It wasn't so difficult to remain out of sight and earshot in this part of the wood; the pines grew densely here, and the fallen needles made a soft pale brown carpet on which my footsteps were silent. The smooth carpet lent a surreal aspect to the wood. The ground rose and fell in mounds and sudden hollows, with scarcely a sharp edge of a stone or a fallen branch left uncovered to break the gently rolling forest floor. Deep in the hollows, horrible bright yellow and red fungi sprouted, Jew's Ear dripped from the sides of sawn-off stumps, and dull russet birds broke cover and fled through the lower branches at my passing.

Ahead of me, the boys didn't notice the startled birds or, if they did, ignored them. They were at home here and deep in their own secret talk.

I thought I had lost them again. Suddenly they were gone. Then I noticed the mound. It rose in a small clearing among the pines, heavily grown over with underbrush. I wondered a little how the shaft came to be here in the wood, so far away from any sort of road. Then I realised that the pine forest was

191

relatively recent, fast growth, planted by men, grafted on to the older woodland further east. A century ago this would have been open land.

I could feel sweat trickling down my back as I neared the mound. Perhaps this was how a hunter felt stalking his prey. Everything around me stood out with unnatural clarity, it was so quiet that I could hear the movements of a large spider on a dry leaf by my shoulder. I began to climb through the bushes on the side of the mound. I inched forward the last few feet and saw the earth curving down into the hole. I wasn't able to see very far down it, the curve of the embrasure was so gradual. Then the sides of the shaft dropped away in a sudden descent into the dark. A root had twisted out of the ground a few feet from the edge and the nylon rope was wound around it like a bright orange snake.

Exactly when I made the decision to cut the rope I couldn't say, but I think something like that had been at the back of my mind ever since I had set out that morning. Almost without thought I reached into my pocket for my penknife and crawling closer to the rope sawed quickly through it, close to the root. As the last threads parted, it slithered away, like something alive, and vanished into the shaft.

I'd expected cries of surprise. Instead, there was only the distant, echoing sound of the rope collapsing onto the shaft floor. There was no other sound after that. Fascinated, I waited. I'd almost decided that I'd made a mistake, that there was no-one down there, when I heard muffled voices, sounding no more than whispers, far below. I began to edge back from the shaft. I reached the edge of the mound and stood up. It was still not too late; even now I could go back and call down to them, tell them what a grand joke it all was. I could get another rope and raise them up. We would all laugh about it. Then they would see that I was not such a dull old uncle as they'd thought but the kind of uncle two mischievous boys could be proud of. How many uncles would have thought of such a grand prank!

## The Pit

Then I heard the first sounds of fear issue from the pit. And suddenly I knew that nobody was ever going to laugh over this. I backed away from the shaft until it was almost hidden in the trees and the voices inaudible. I began to walk very quickly back to the house.

For a week or so the fuss surrounding our house was almost unendurable. Police and reporters took turns banging on the front door, and all the men of the neighbouring farms and houses turned out in a touching show of support to help search for the boys. The police brought dogs, but the animals were mainly interested in the trail of aniseed that I'd put down the first evening of the boys disappearance, when ostensibly I'd been out hunting for them myself.

After ten days most of the media interest died away; people have short attention spans, and there was a propitious air crash at Heathrow which distracted attention. Martha was inconsolable, but reconciled to never seeing either of them alive again. Alex was more embarrassed by all the fuss, I thought, than anything else, and took to working even longer hours at the office. Only a solitary, sad-faced police detective remained upon the scene, hanging onto the case with limpet-like tenacity. One afternoon he called at the house and asked if I had a half hour to spare. Both Martha and Alex were out. "There's something I'd like your opinion on," he said.

He led me down through the garden and into the trees; I felt my breath tightening as we took the path toward the mine shaft. Then he branched off and for a short while I lost my bearings until we came out near the ploughed field with the scarecrow.

"I wondered if you could tell me anything about this," he said, pointing to one of the fence posts.

Someone had nailed a dog to the post. Three nails had been driven through its neck, a fourth through its lower paws, pinning them together. Its forelegs jutted stiffly out towards us. So this was what they'd wanted the nails for. I stepped back and looked along the line of fence posts. There were more of them; I saw rabbits, magpies, several rats, a cat; a row of petty crucifixions. I imagined the boys dragging the animals through the grass, hammering in the nails. I couldn't imagine why they'd done it, unless it was to satisfy some sadistic childish instinct; there was something very deliberate about the way the long nails had been driven through the animals' throats, genitals, or eyes, when a piece of wire looped around their necks would have done the job equally well.

"Pretty little scene, isn't it?" the detective said.

"Yes, but I've seen this sort of thing before. Farmers do it to scare off pests. I think it's more dramatic than effective. Why did you ask me to look at this, Inspector?"

"Farmers don't usually nail up dogs and cats. It was one of the farmers helping in the search who noticed it. We know the boys played in this area, and we wondered if you could tell us anything?"

"You're trying to build up a psychological profile of them, is that it?"

The detective pulled out an enormous chequered handkerchief and blew his nose noisily. "If we know how they spent their time, and where, then we'll have a better idea where to concentrate the search. This is the first real lead we've had."

"I'm afraid you know as much about this as I do," I told him.

Looking across the row of poles with their grisly trophies to the scarecrow nodding in the wind, I had a sense of something almost primal, as if these fence posts had become totem poles set up to honour this ragged god of the field. Again I had that feeling of being watched, of someone behind me. But there was only the policeman and myself here; the only other figure in sight was that of the scarecrow on the slope of the field. Nevertheless, I was glad to get away from there and back home to the security of my study.

Interest in the search died down. Within days, the searchers were reduced to a few scattered groups of tired looking policemen. I thought the sad-faced detective had given up or been recalled, but out walking, I noticed his car parked in a lane, and another time I saw him studying something in the middle of the ploughed field.

One evening he asked me, "Have you any ideas why they would want to run off?" I'd met him in the lane near the gate. He had a casual way of talking, as if he was merely a neighbour passing the time of day. I had the impression that he was tired of the whole business and was just looking for an excuse to call it a day.

"As a matter of fact," I said, "I have. But I've kept it to myself because I was afraid of disturbing their parents even more."

"Not wanting to seem facetious, sir, but their parents already think they're dead."

"Oh yes, I think they might well be. It's possible anyway. It's just the reason that I think they ran away might cause more upset."

"What reason would that be, sir?"

"Well, this is all pure speculation, understand. But they were very close, for young boys. Extremely close. One might even say intimate."

"You're suggesting that they might have run away together, like a couple of lovers?"

"If you want to put it that way. I thought it best not to say anything. You know what the media would make of something like this. It would finish poor Martha."

"Very considerate of you, I'm sure, sir. You needn't worry; I'll be certain to keep it to myself. No need to upset people unnecessarily. But we'll bear what you've said in mind, you can be sure."

"Does that mean you'll be spreading your search farther afield?"

He looked at his shoes for a moment then smiled at me. "All things in good time, sir," he said. He turned away, then paused, and looked back at me. "I understand that you're not a married man, sir."

"That's right. I don't see that that's got anything to do with this."

"As you say, sir." He walked away down the lane to his car.

The next morning I looked up from my desk to see him in the garden; he was looking up at the house with a thoughtful expression on his face. I knew then that he was not going to go away. Not unless I led him.

It was obvious that I would have to do something to lead them away from the area. They could probably search for months and still never find the shaft; it was easily overlooked, even from a few feet away. But the risk seemed unnecessary if there was a way to lure them off. I had an idea, but I kept putting it off. It meant going back to the shaft. At last, reluctantly, I went.

Carrying the rope was a problem which I solved by winding it around my waist under a loose pullover. I set out a little after midday; to go at night would have invited suspicion. The woods were as silent as they had been the day that I'd followed the boys that last time. It seemed impossible to believe that that had been only two weeks ago. When I reached the shaft, I quickly removed my outer clothes, rolled them up and tucked them out of sight under a bush. I secured the rope firmly to the root and in my vest and underpants, with a loose feeling in my bowels; I began the descent of the shaft. I had no idea how deep it was. Not more than forty feet though; that was the length of the rope they'd used.

I suppose I'd expected some awful smell, but there was only the close musty odour of the earth and damp air enclosed in the shaft. A human being can survive only two or three days without water, but almost two weeks without food. Supposing that there was water down there? Suppose they were still alive? I pushed the fear down; even if they were alive, they'd hardly be in any condition to present a threat to me. My feet touched bottom and immediately one of my questions was answered. I had stepped into thick slippery mud. I turned and shone the torch around quickly, then looked at the ground. The mud was starting to dry out and crack at the edges; in some places holes had been scooped in it, the way that animals will dig for water. In the end, though, they had been out of luck; it hadn't rained in three weeks. I raised the torch and looked around more carefully.

I was in a small cavern reaching away about twenty or thirty feet. The end of the cavern was a jumble of rocks; at some point there must have been a fall which had sealed it off from the network of other shafts. Another smaller tunnel led off from the right hand wall. I shone the torch down it. The boys were there, propped against another fall of rocks. I suppose it had been the warmest part of the cave.

They lay huddled together like a pair of lovers, arms around one another's necks. Edward lay with his face against James's chest, and James's gaze seemed to dare me to approach. Although I knew they were dead, it was some time before I could bring myself to approach. The next few minutes were the worst of my life. It was necessary to strip the boys' bodies of every article of clothing they wore. It would have been no good stealing clothes from the boys' rooms, because Martha had furnished the police with a detailed description of what they had been wearing that last day. It was an awkward job, and was made worse by the stiffness of their limbs. There is something utterly repellent about handling dead human flesh, its coldness and lack of elasticity; but finally I finished the job. Tying the clothes in a bundle, I backed out of the tunnel. The boys' naked white shapes lay tumbled over one another at the end of the tunnel like abandoned shop window mannequins. Within moments I was climbing back up the rope towards the green eye of the shaft opening, under the trees.

It was late afternoon when I reached the cliffs two miles north of the wood. Perhaps it's only in Cornwall that you find this bizarre juxtaposition of woods, fields and heath opening onto the sea. In a grassy hollow, I placed the bundle of clothes by a large rock. I was confident that the clothes would soon be discovered; this cliff-side walk was popular with courting couples. As I stood up, the muffling effect of the hollow was lost and I heard the booming of the waves on the narrow beach far below.

I began my journey home. I was reasonably confident that as soon as the clothes were found and identified, any coroner would have to return an open verdict on the boys. Perhaps they had hidden the clothes, gone swimming, and been swept away by the treacherous tides along this coast; more romantic hearts would imagine them stepping off the cliff hand in hand, bodies again swept under by the tide. Or perhaps some evildoer had done away with them. I was genuinely sorry that I had had to kill the boys, but I could not feel sorry that they were dead. I wished only that their lives had been snuffed out by some unfeeling natural destructive force; but, failing that, I had done what they had compelled me to.

I realised that my route home was taking me through the ploughed fields along the eastern edge of the wood. High up in the sloping field, the scarecrow hung wretchedly from its pole. I couldn't help thinking that it was a pretty ineffectual sort of protection; a crow even now rested upon one of its shoulders and pecked at the hollowed turnip head. As I looked away, the head turned fractionally.

It was such a slight movement that, if my senses had not been in such a heightened state, magnified through stress, I might not have noticed it. Then I realised that the head had shifted from the pecking of the crow, and I repeated that several times in my thoughts. Only the crow. The crow pecking at the head. It had not really turned to look at me.

I reached the edge of the field and leaned briefly against the stile there, but I was reluctant to stop; it must be getting late by now. The sun was already low over the horizon. I climbed the stile and glanced back and saw that the pole was now standing skeletal and bare in the centre of the field. Sunlight bathed the field in a hard white light. Shiny stones, quartz and mica, gave off brilliant sparks as if the field was an expanse of glittering water, the ploughed furrows like frozen waves. And something was swimming out there in the middle of the field. It moved like a swimmer in difficulty. Crows flocked around it, jostling to peck at its head. I ran home.

That was yesterday. I was exhausted when I got home and went straight to bed. I dreamed that I was back on that lonely beach, looking down at marks in the sand. They were strange marks, a central furrow with odd scrabblings upon either side. I followed them into a cave, where I saw something hunched on the floor. I thought it was a seal, but when I got close I saw that it was just a bundle of rags and sticks. Some of the rags looked familiar; they were the boys' clothes. I tried to pick them up, but the bundle suddenly unfolded and loomed over me, and it was the scarecrow grinning with rotten black marrow lips and reaching for my throat with its fingers of long twigs.

Martha and Alex were gone when I got home yesterday; I found a note saying that Martha couldn't stand being here now that she was sure the boys would never come home again.

I'm sure that the sad-faced detective knows something. He's waiting for me to make a mistake; if I go out for a drive he'll be somewhere along the route watching. If I drove farther than the village I know he'd quickly radio for road blocks. It doesn't matter though because I'm not going to panic; I won't run. I'm going to stay right here. I can handle the dreams. They can't frighten me by daylight. Anyway, the old place needs someone to look after it. Martha's only been gone one day, and already the casual help are getting slack. Some fool has left a great bundle of twigs and rags in the middle of the drive, near the door. I suppose that I'd better go down and clear it up. I'll do it in just a little while; there's plenty of time. It won't hurt anyone, lying there, after all.

Lightning Source UK Ltd.
Milton Keynes UK
UKOW051808140212

187312UK00001B/4/P